One Weird Day at
FREEKHAM HIGH
THUMB

Other books in the series

Sock
Ouch!
Pigeon

One Weird Day at
FREEKHAM HIGH
THUMB

Steve Cole

OXFORD
UNIVERSITY PRESS

OXFORD
UNIVERSITY PRESS

Great Clarendon Street, Oxford OX2 6DP

Oxford University Press is a department of the University of Oxford.
It furthers the University's objective of excellence in research, scholarship,
and education by publishing worldwide in

Oxford New York

Auckland Cape Town Dar es Salaam Hong Kong Karachi
Kuala Lumpur Madrid Melbourne Mexico City Nairobi
New Delhi Shanghai Taipei Toronto

With offices in

Argentina Austria Brazil Chile Czech Republic France Greece
Guatemala Hungary Italy Japan Poland Portugal Singapore
South Korea Switzerland Thailand Turkey Ukraine Vietnam

Oxford is a registered trade mark of Oxford University Press
in the UK and in certain other countries

British Library Cataloguing in Publication Data

Data available

ISBN-13: 978-0-19-275424-6
ISBN-10: 0-19-275424-6

1 3 5 7 9 10 8 6 4 2

Typeset by Palimpsest Book Production Limited,
Polmont, Stirlingshire

Printed in Great Britain by Cox & Wyman, Reading, Berkshire

For Jill, the big thumbs-up in my life

Registration

There were three things that Sam Innocent didn't expect that first May morning at Freekham High.

The first unexpected thing: that it could actually be hotter inside the school than outside. He'd just shoved his way through a seething, sweat-soaked scrum of kids in the sun-baked playground, braving the *Who's he?* stares and consoling himself that at least it would be cooler in the entrance hall.

Fat chance. It was like walking into an oven in a sauna in a greenhouse in the Sahara Desert. Maybe a little hotter. Which was weird, since Freekham High *looked* as if it should be cold, from the outside anyway. It was stern and scary looking: a bundle of blocks, all glass and steel and concrete, sharp angles and low ceilings— mercilessly modern. 'A progressive school', according to the sign outside.

1

Sam knew that loads of schools made this claim. Thanks to his dad's ever-relocating job, he got to enjoy the first day of school roughly two or three times a year. At first, he'd thought 'progressive' meant they had air-conditioning, cool computers, and stuff like that. Uh-uh. Each new school was progressively *worse* than the last, true, but Sam wasn't convinced that counted.

The second unexpected thing was the girl.

There she stood beneath the sign SCHOOL OFFICE with her back to him. Her blonde hair straggled down to the middle of her back, even as she stooped over a table to fill in some kind of form.

Sam sauntered over to join her there. REPORT TO THE SCHOOL OFFICE UPON ARRIVAL AT 8.30 a.m., the letter confirming his enrolment had screamed in black capitals. As a new starter he guessed he'd have forms to fill in like blondie here. Maybe he could ask to borrow her pen; that could be a good way of saying hello . . .

When he was halfway across the hall an alarm started blaring, as if he'd tripped some invisible beam between the whitewashed walls or trodden on a pressure pad in the fake wood flooring. It sounded halfway between a police siren and an angry goose with a throat infection. Seconds later, the hall was thronging with noisy, complaining kids, traipsing along to their classrooms on autopilot. They looked like hundreds of resigned prisoners, all in regulation green and white, trooping back to their cells after a brief taste of freedom.

Sam held still in the middle of the flow. Aside from one or two curious glances he was largely ignored. The girl was attracting far more attention, particularly from the boys.

At last the crowds passed from the hall. While the final stragglers loped out of sight down the corridors to registration, Sam continued his sweaty odyssey over to the school office. He caught sight of his reflection in the glass of a picture frame as he approached; enough to see his damp fringe was sticking up from his freckled forehead like a black spiky tiara. He plucked at it worriedly, trying to smooth it back down—just as the girl turned to face him.

She was the striking kind. In many ways the two of them were opposites; her eyes were wide and watery blue, his were oval and brown. Her nose was straight as a ski slope, his was short

 3

and snub. Sam was usually considered quite tall for a thirteen year old, but this girl matched him inch for inch.

'Hi,' he said. 'My name's Sam. Sam Innocent.'

She raised an eyebrow. 'Till proved guilty?'

His smile sagged, and she noticed.

'People say that a lot, huh?'

'Only one or two million times.'

'Thought so.' She clicked her tongue. 'So with all that practice, why haven't you worked out some smart comeback?'

'My mum taught me it's rude to devastate someone with your wit till you know their name.'

She smiled at that. 'Sara Knot,' she offered.

'Not what?'

She turned back to her form, shrugging a cascade of hair back over her shoulder. 'Not heard that one a million times either.'

'So now we're even?'

Sara didn't answer, intent on whatever she was writing. Sam wiped fresh sweat from his brow and peered over her shoulder. She was filling in a new pupil registration form.

'Hey!' he said, amazed, as he read. 'I'm starting here today too!'

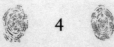

She looked at him suspiciously. 'In the middle of May?'

'It's a rubbish time to start, isn't it?' he said. 'Everyone in the whole school's cosy in their cliques and gangs. Someone new turns up, spends a month trying to get accepted . . .'

She nodded wearily. 'Then it's summer. Nice long, lonely holidays.'

'Right!' he beamed. 'And in September, you show your hopeful face but everyone's forgotten you. You have to start all over again.' He blew out a long sigh of relief. 'Thought it would just be me!'

'Whoop-de-doo,' said Sara drily. 'We can maybe form, like, a loser's club.'

His eyes widened as he scanned her form again. 'I don't believe it—we even have the same birthday!'

She looked at him sharply from under her fringe. 'Yeah, as if. February 29th?'

'We do!' he protested. 'The same year and everything!'

'Seriously?' She looked a bit weirded out. 'What are the chances of that happening?'

'Especially when we're both starting at this

dump right at exactly the same time,' Sam agreed, feeling kind of freaked himself.

This was the third unexpected thing.

'Maybe it's a sign,' Sam reasoned. 'A sign that we should, you know, stick together . . .'

He'd meant it to sound friendly, but Sara's eyes narrowed.

'OK, I get it,' she said. 'Ha, ha, very funny. You can stop now.' She peered about over his shoulder. 'Where are your friends hiding? Or did they wet themselves laughing already?'

'Huh?'

'All this "Hey, we're exactly the same!" stuff . . . So, what, you're the big school joker, right? Here to make fun of the new girl?'

'No! It's all true!' Sam held up his hands. 'I'm innocent!'

Sara folded her arms. 'Till proved guilty.'

He scowled. 'Once I've got one of those forms to fill in I'll prove it to you.' He peered through the office window but the receptionist was busy on the phone the other side of the counter. 'Why are you so uptight, anyway?'

'This is the second school I've had to start at this year,' Sara informed him. 'Last year I went to *three*.'

'*Me too!*' He couldn't help bursting in. 'That kind of coincidence is incredible—'

'So,' she continued heavily, 'I'm kind of used to being an easy target for creeps like you!'

Sam stared at her in speechless disbelief. Admittedly, he *had* often been labelled the noisy, jokey one in class—the boy who gave cheek to teachers in return for detentions. At least you made an impression that way. Plus you didn't have to worry about no one talking to you when you were locked up all lunchtime and couldn't talk anyway.

'And I thought I was paranoid about starting new schools!' he finally managed.

'So go get the form and prove you're not a lying scumbag,' said Sara, hands on hips.

'Fine!' Sam turned to peer in at the woman in the office. She looked to be in her fifties, with a face full of fake tan and wrinkles. 'Excuse me?' he called, leaning in over the counter—then realized she was still on the phone. She was talking about having an operation or something . . . He drummed his fingers on the countertop, hoping Sara wouldn't finish her form and push off before he could start on his own.

The woman hung up at last. Mopping her shiny brow with a hanky, she turned to him with an apologetic smile. 'Sorry to leave you waiting, lovey.'

'No problem!' Sam gave her his most winning smile—Sara needed to see he was a nice guy. 'Not your fault you're left to run things single-handed, is it?'

The receptionist pursed her lips and he heard a sharp intake of breath from Sara. She was giving him a look of pure horror.

Bemused, Sam tried to back-pedal. 'Not that you couldn't cope here with one hand tied behind your back, I'm sure.'

Sara groaned, shaking her head at him desperately, while the receptionist gave him a stony look.

'Uh, may I have a new pupil registration form, please, if you have one to hand?' Sam asked meekly. He turned to Sara, who now looked almost amused. *What?* he mouthed.

The receptionist slapped down a piece of paper on the desk and slid it over to him.

'That was quick!' he beamed. 'I have to hand it to you, you . . .'

Uh-oh.

. . . you only have one hand, he realized with a sinking feeling. The other was a smooth, pink plastic fake, pressing down on his form.

Great. A *fourth* unexpected thing. He hadn't seen *that* coming. From now on, he decided he would try to expect the unexpected at Freekham High—a modern, progressive, and clearly completely FREAKY school.

Sam shoehorned a sheepish smile between his crimson cheeks. 'Er, sorry to mention . . . hands . . . like that,' he told the receptionist, gingerly pulling the paper away from her falsie fingers. 'Erm, you don't have a pen handy—' he winced— 'do you?'

The receptionist produced a chewed biro and passed it to him. Then she stalked off to the other side of her little office.

Sam closed his eyes. 'Ouch. How many times did I say "hand" in the last sixty seconds?'

'Too many to count on her plastic fingers, anyway.' Sara burst out into slightly horsey sniggers. 'OK, I'm convinced. That was too painful to be a put on. You just arrived here.'

'And the first thing I've learned at Freekham

 9

High? Keep your hands to yourself.' He filled in his date of birth on the form first, making sure Sara could see it.

'That really is weird, isn't it,' she murmured.

'So I'm not a lying scumbag?'

'Not a lying one, anyway,' she conceded. But Sam saw her pale blue eyes sparkle as she said it.

Once the questionnaires were filled in, the receptionist gave Sara and Sam a starter's pack—or more accurately, a few bits of card and paper in a dusty plastic bag—and pointed them in the direction of a far distant classroom. By now, neither of them was very surprised to learn they'd been placed in the same form group.

'There's full school assembly each Monday morning,' the receptionist explained to Sara. 'That's where everyone will be by now, but you don't want to be doing with that on your first day. You'll see from your timetable that your first lesson's double Chemistry, in your form room. Just find your way to Mr Penter's lab and wait for everyone to come back from the main hall.'

That was their mission. But it was turning out to be harder than expected.

'Looks like there's a few laboratories,' said Sara, scrutinizing a clumsily folded photocopied plan of the various school buildings. 'All in one block.' At the end of a long, long corridor, they took a right turn which led to the world outside. After a minute panting in the strengthening sunshine, they reached another block, and Sara led the way down a long, roasting corridor paved with gleaming tiles. 'I think it's this way.'

Sara wished it wasn't so hot. Sweat was tickling the roots of her long, thick hair, and her cheeks felt as if they were glowing neon red. But besides the temperature, there was something about Freekham High that left her feeling oddly edgy. Maybe it was something to do with the smell of the place. Like most other schools, there was a definite, almost comforting whiff of disinfectant, chalk dust, and gym shoes about the corridors . . . but Sara was picking up something else too. She felt an air of great age and mustiness about the place, weirdly at odds with its modern appearance.

You're imagining it, she told herself.

'Everything in this welcome pack bangs on about the "exciting autumn term ahead",' Sam grumbled, sorting through the drab contents of his goody bag. 'They're eight months late! They ought to update it for people like us.'

'Maybe they're actually four months early,' Sara suggested, 'and we're the very first to be welcomed to *this* year's exciting autumn term ahead.'

'Maybe,' said Sam, unconvinced.

Sara frowned. 'I was being saracastic. You got that, right?'

'Duh!' Sam retorted, hoping she'd think his blushes were down to the sweltering heat. 'Of course I did.'

'And you know what else?' She paused, angled the photocopy. 'This map is rubbish.'

'Probably out of date. I bet they've changed everything round since September.'

'That's progressive schools for you.' Sara turned the map upside down, hoping it would make more sense.

'Maybe the receptionist gave us a bogus map,' said Sam.

'What, she rustled one up in revenge? In under a minute?'

'Fastest hand in the west?'

'Don't start that again. I thought she seemed nice.'

'Nice?' Sam stared at her, appalled. '*Nice?* Look, receptionists may not be actual teachers, but they're from the same stock. Anyone who would actually choose to work in a school has *issues*. Stands to reason they take their problems out on us.'

'Well, let the taking out commence.' She sighed, and turned up her nose at the faint tang of chemicals. 'I think our new classroom's just down here.'

She led them through an archway into a short, red-bricked passageway that led on to a set of silver double doors. SCIENCE BLOCK had been daubed in futuristic writing on a rocket-shaped sign that hung down from the ceiling.

'Impressive,' said Sam wryly.

But before they could go inside, the doors burst outwards and two boys emerged, struggling to hold a large cardboard box upright between them. One of the kids was broad, blond, and baby-faced, with red, ruddy cheeks. His mate was tall and rangy, hook-nosed and shifty looking. They staggered past, panting with sweaty effort.

13

'Need any help?' asked Sara.

'No,' snapped the tall boy, quickly. 'Get lost.'

Sam shrugged. 'We did that already.'

The boy just scowled and quickened his step. His baby-faced mate squealed as he was forced to trot along faster.

'Well, he was a real charmer,' said Sara. 'I thought everyone was in assembly?'

Sam shrugged. 'Probably bunking off.'

They went through into the whiffy science block to locate their classroom. Filled with first day nerves and bravado, neither of them gave the boys with the box another thought.

But that would soon change.

Periods One and Two
Chemistry

'This must be it,' Sara said, pushing open a heavy wooden door. 'Our form room.'

The classroom was big and grey and predictable. Like any chemistry lab it was filled with acid-scarred tables arranged in clusters of three, porcelain sinks, wooden stools, and cupboards full of chemicals.

'Nice of them to lay out the red carpet for us.' Sam leaned against the nearest table. 'God, I hate this bit.'

Sara nodded. 'The freak show. Everyone staring, whispering to their mates . . .'

'Laughing . . .'

She gave him a look. 'You get laughed at?'

Sam cleared his throat. 'Uh . . . When I make, like, a brilliant joke, I mean.'

'Right,' said Sara, giving him the benefit of the doubt. She could tell he was nervous—it was hot, sure, but he was sweating so badly he could be a human sprinkler.

She hardly felt cool herself. In fact, her insides were wriggling like a ferret in a box. A distant tide of scuffling feet and chatter was slowly rising; assembly was over and the day's first lesson about to begin.

'Stand by,' murmured Sam, joining her in the middle of the classroom. 'It's showtime.'

Sara smoothed out her hair and bit her lip. Moments later the lab was invaded by a sweaty throng, and looks were soon shooting Sara's way like laser beams. She wanted to crawl into a cupboard and hide, but she couldn't let anyone see that. Instead she forced herself to meet their stares and carefully put on her New Girl face.

· She'd nervously practised this face in front of the mirror a million times—it wasn't an easy look to crack. She couldn't look too smiley, or people would think she was a spaced-out freak. But she couldn't look too sullen either, or she would be labelled a moody cow—when really, she was pretty easy-going. Ideally, the message that New Girl face gave out was in the ballpark of *I'm-quite-approachable-and-fun-once-you-get-to-*

16

know-me-so-please-don't-shun-me-as-a-loser-before-I've-even-opened-my-mouth.

Sam glanced at her. 'Are you all right?' he hissed. 'You look like you've got wind.'

'Thanks for the confidence boost,' said Sara, scowling.

But then a girl walked in, straggling behind the rest of the class, and Sara's look became one of astonishment.

The girl was a tall, pencil-thin skinhead with a white, rounded face. Her eyes were a flinty sea-green between eyelashes like black fronds, and her straight nose pointed down like an arrow to the red lipsticky slash of her mouth. Everything about her screamed attitude—her looks, the way she walked, the way everything she wore was slightly askew—and yet to Sara's surprise, the girl smiled across at her and Sam with what seemed like real warmth. There was a mischievous look in her eyes as she took her place at the very back of the room.

Slowly, the class took their seats, while Sara and Sam stayed stuck in the middle of the room. There were just two empty places. One was beside the skinhead girl at the back. The other was at the front beside that chubby blond boy she and Sam had passed as they'd entered the science block. Back then Sara had mentally tagged him *harmless*, but now she came to observe him in his natural habitat she could see she'd been way too polite.

This kid was *sucking his thumb*! *Really* sucking it. Not just chewing a nail or biting a wart or something—this was real down-to-the-knuckle suction.

'Pack it in, Ashley,' said a burly girl sitting opposite him. 'You're gonna make me hurl.'

But Ashley sucked on, apparently unbothered by the thought of experiencing the girl's breakfast at first hand. He stared straight ahead as if he was in a trance. Apart from a few filthy looks, no one else nearby even reacted, so Sara could only assume that this was everyday behaviour. Eeuw!

Sam leaned over to Sara. 'Toss you for the seat next to baby boy,' he hissed.

'No way,' said Sara. 'He puts the "freak" into Freekham! I'll take my chances with the skinhead, thanks.'

'See what teacher has to say about that.' Sam

murmured, nodding to the door. 'Enter Mr Penter!'

The noise in the classroom dipped as an imposing man with short, neatly combed brown hair came inside. He had a patchy beard and the reddest eyes Sara had ever seen—as if he'd been up all night reading newspapers through the wrong end of a telescope.

'Ah. The newcomers,' he said gruffly, squinting at Sam and Sara. 'I'm Mr Penter, I'll be your form tutor. Welcome to Freekham High.'

'And you *are* welcome to it,' chimed some comedian behind Sara, to much laughter.

'That's enough,' snapped Penter. 'Now then, newcomers—kindly introduce yourselves to the class.'

Sam beamed around the room. 'Sam Innocent.'

'Innocent?' Penter smiled, revealing a row of yellowing tombstones. 'Innocent till proven—?'

'That's the one, sir,' said Sam quickly, with a smile as fake as the receptionist's tan. 'Very quick of you.'

Penter glowered at the interruption. 'And you, miss . . . ?'

'Sara Knot,' said Sara.

19

'Knot!' Penter gave a snort of laughter. 'Not what, may I ask?'

Sam sighed noisily.

Sara smiled at Penter sweetly. 'Well, sir, in order of most frequently quoted: Sara Knot-a-lot, Knot on your nelly, Knot in a million years, Knot what I've heard, Knot today thank you—'

'Sara,' Sam chided. 'Knot in front of Mr Penter!'

The whole class erupted in laughter. Even Ashley chortled, his lip-grip slipping slightly on his pruney thumb. Sara tried to hide her own smile, because Penter's face was darkening fast.

'Quite the double act, aren't you?' he said tightly, checking some notes on his desk. 'Born on the same day, starting here on the same day . . .' He fixed them both with a steely stare. 'Well, luckily for you, I'm feeling generous this morning. I'm prepared to put your behaviour down to first day nerves—on the understanding that from now on you'll be model pupils.'

'Yes, sir,' said Sara, and Sam nodded.

'Sara, take a seat beside Memphis Ball,' Penter went on. Sara frowned for a moment—was that an event or a name?—until she saw the skinny skinhead girl flick up a beckoning finger in her direction.

She smiled at Sam. 'Unlucky,' she whispered, and crossed a little nervously to her seat.

Memphis Ball watched her coolly like a cat as she approached. 'Sam and Sara, huh?' she murmured. 'Born on the same day?'

'29th February,' Sara nodded.

'Kind of weird you both show up here together,' said Memphis. 'Any other freaky coincidences?'

Sara frowned. 'Maybe. Why?'

Memphis widened her eyes. 'Fate plays some funny tricks,' she said mysteriously.

Before Sara could ask her what she meant, Penter flashed a warning glance in her direction. 'Now, Mr Innocent—you'll be sitting next to Ashley Lamb.'

Sam bowed his head like a condemned prisoner and took his seat. Ashley didn't even seem to notice.

'Aww, sweet,' sneered the burly girl. 'Sucker's got himself a new thumb-chum!'

'Who's that?' asked Sara quietly.

'Ruth Cook,' said Memphis. 'About as bright

as a nightlight bulb covered by a cushion. Also known as Ruthless Cook.'

'Because she's a mean hand with a frying pan?'

'Not unless she's hitting someone with it. Best avoided.'

Penter pulled a pile of papers from his desk drawer. 'Today we'll continue our work on the Periodic Table. Innocent, can you tell us what the Periodic table is?'

Sam made a great show of thinking hard. 'It's a table that's only used every now and then?'

A few laughs, a few groans from the class. Penter's face grew darker still.

'That boy is trying way too hard,' commented Memphis.

'Or just trying, full stop,' smiled Sara.

'Innocent, I don't know if your flippant approach to lessons was tolerated at your last school,' said Penter gravely, 'but it will not be here. Now, collect these worksheets and hand them out to everyone in the class.'

'Yes, sir,' said Sam, slouching over to take the worksheets. 'Like a model pupil, sir.' He grudgingly passed out one or two of the papers—but the moment Penter turned his back to scrawl on

 22

the chalkboard, Sam struck a cheesy pose beside Ruth Cook, shielding his eyes and looking into the distance.

'Hi,' he told her, 'I'm a "catalogue model" pupil.'

She plucked a paper from the pile and gave him a sour look. 'Pack it in.'

Penter glanced their way. Instantly, Sam continued passing out the papers perfectly normally: to the girl next to Ruth who was meek and mousy, to a dozy-looking lad with ginger hair . . . But the second Penter turned back to his chalkboard, Sam strutted over to Sara's table with his chest out and his head in the air, to a few muffled titters.

Memphis held out her hand for a paper, her face straight but her incredible eyes amused. '"Catwalk model" pupil, right?'

'In my dreams,' he grinned, passing one worksheet to her and one to Sara.

'Just be careful,' Memphis told him. 'Penter's not one you push too far.'

But Sam had already set off for the next table, this time holding out his arms like he was flying—a model plane pupil. He was getting some titters from the class, but most people were frowning and whispering and tapping their heads like they thought he was mental.

Exasperated by this latest disturbance, Penter turned round to face his pupils with a fierce gummy grimace.

Sam bailed out of his imaginary plane and walked innocently across to the next group of tables in the centre of the room. But suddenly, with a squawk of surprise, he went flying backwards as if he'd stepped on a banana skin. The worksheets slipped from his fingers and fell flapping all around like giant confetti as he knocked into the back of the guy sitting behind him.

In turn, with a loud 'Oof!' the boy fell sideways into the girl with bunches next to him.

She shrieked and pitched forwards from her stool, crashing into Sara and Memphis's table as she fell, pushing it backwards.

Memphis jumped up but Sara was a second too slow. With a yelp, she overbalanced on her stool and smacked the back of her head against the wall before collapsing to the floor in a dazed heap.

For a second, there was a deadly hush. Then the classroom broke out into noisy, rapturous applause.

'Are you all right?' asked Memphis, helping Sara back up.

'I'll let you know when the room's stopped spinning,' she groaned.

'Samuel Innocent!' roared Penter, and the joyful class fell silent. Sara could only imagine the look of scandal on the teacher's face—her vision was still too blurred. 'What is the meaning of this disturbance?'

'I slipped, sir!' said Sam indignantly.

'You doofus!' snarled a boy, presumably the one Sam had hit.

'I could've killed myself!' added the incredible flying girl, somewhat melodramatically.

'I'm sorry, OK?' said Sam. 'It wasn't my fault, there's a puddle here on the floor!'

'Don't be so ridiculous, boy!' thundered Penter. 'This floor was as dry as a bone at registration! I walked all over it.'

'It's true!' cried Sam. 'Look!'

Sara squinted to see, but couldn't pull anything into focus.

'If there's a puddle there, then it's a puddle of your own making!' Penter snapped.

'Ugh, gross!' hooted Ruth Cook. 'New boy wet himself!'

A tidal wave of laughter roared across the classroom.

'It's icy water!' shouted Sam. Sara watched blearily as he got up, rubbing his back where he fell. 'Look, there's crushed ice there. Where would I get—'

'You were standing close to that spot before the rest of us arrived from assembly,' said Penter. 'You and your fellow newcomer—'

''Scuse, sir,' said Memphis, 'Sara's done her head in. There's a big lump.'

Penter glowered over resentfully. 'All right,' he sighed. 'Come here, Sara, and I'll take a look.'

Sara walked over to his desk, feeling a little wobbly.

'Well, you two, this is hardly the most auspicious start to your time at Freekham High,' Penter said gravely. 'Innocent—you've just earned yourself a detention. You'll join Mr Lamb in staying behind at breaktime.'

Sam stared at him in outrage. 'But, sir—!'

'No buts.'

'Apart from mine getting an unfair kicking,' grumbled Sam.

'Finish handing out the papers then clean up that mess,' Penter ordered. 'Or you'll be back here at lunchtime too!'

As Sam skulked off to the paper towel dispenser beside the fumes cabinet, Penter turned Sara around and tapped his finger on the back of her head.

'Ow!' she complained.

'Hasn't broken the skin, but you've got quite a swelling,' said Penter. 'I suppose you'd better get yourself down to the school nurse. He has a room by the school office. Can you find your way there?'

Sara nodded and winced. 'I think so.'

Ten minutes later and hopelessly lost, Sara was regretting going it alone. Every corridor looked the same, and it felt as if an elephant was trampolining in her head. The heat wasn't helping either. Her scalp prickled with sweat more than ever and she had to fight against waves of dizziness. The siren went to mark the end of period one, and reminded her of what a marvellous start she'd made at Freekham High.

Finally, she staggered out into the entrance hall where she'd first arrived. There was the school office—so the nurse must be close by.

Sara made her way over to the office. The receptionist might only have one hand, but hopefully it was of the helping variety.

However, the only person in the office was a younger, big-boned woman with all digits intact, growing out a frizzy perm. She was mopping at her shiny forehead with a tissue.

Sara leaned on the counter outside the office window and frowned. 'Am I hallucinating or have you had a make-over since registration?'

'I'm just a temp,' she smiled, her voice high, bright, and—to Sara—extremely painful. 'The real receptionist's got a clinic appointment or something . . . Can I help?'

'Do you know where the school nurse is?' Sara asked. 'Teacher sent me. My head hurts.'

The temp gave her a sympathetic smile and wiped her forehead. 'Probably this heat.'

'Actually, it was a wall.'

'Making them drop like flies this morning, it is,' said the temp, not listening 'School nurse is out of this hall and through the first door on your right. Though you might have to form a queue!'

Sara went to investigate, struggling against a tide of students on their way to their next lessons.

At last she reached the door, and knocked. There was a sudden scraping, scuffling noise from inside, but no invitation to come in.

'Hello?' she called.

More scuffling. Footsteps on the floor. What was going on?

She tried the door handle and peered inside. It was a small room painted regulation school beige. A desk and chair sat before an open window, surrounded by cabinets, a mini-fridge-freezer, shelves full of books, and a large porcelain sink.

But no nurse. Only some guy maybe a year or two older than her. He was lying on a couch as if he'd just been caught out—red-faced and wide eyed. Sara felt he looked vaguely familiar, but couldn't think where from. Whatever, for some reason he looked incredibly relieved to see her.

'Everything OK here?' she asked.

'I'm Roger,' he announced as if this explained everything. He craned his neck as if expecting someone else to appear behind her. 'What are you doing here?'

'I came to see the nurse. Where is he?'

'He went to the bog.'

'That's nice.'

Roger sat up a little way. 'What did you do, anyway?'

'I fell and hurt my head.'

'Heat too much for you, huh?'

She closed her eyes wearily. 'How about you?'

'Uh . . . ankle,' Roger said, waving his left leg. 'Yeah, my ankle. It's really sore. Really swollen.'

'Bummer. My gran's ankles swell up in the heat, too.'

'It wasn't the heat! I got it, er . . . I got it playing football.' He looked past her at the door again.

He seemed kind of anxious.

'It's OK,' she said. 'I believe you.'

'What?' he said, still flustered. 'Well, you *should* believe me. 'Cause it's the truth.' He swung his legs round and perched on the side of the

30

couch. 'Hey, I just realized—I left my bag outside the office on my way here. Could you go and get it for me? Quickly?'

'I just came from there. I didn't see a bag.'

'It's black and red. Check for me?' He shook his leg feebly. 'Please?'

'OK,' Sara said. 'I guess I can do that even with major concussion . . .'

She turned and stalked off back to the office. Big-bones was there, gassing on the phone while she fanned herself with a notebook. But there was no sign of a bag either inside or out.

For a moment she thought she might wait and ask the temp receptionist. Then she decided she was already going over and above the call of duty, trailing over here with head injuries for some guy who wasn't even that cute. So Sara went back to the nurse's room and threw open the door. 'Sorry, Roger, no sign of your bag. Maybe it melted in the—'

'Can I help you?'

Sara jumped. A young Asian man was looking at her oddly. 'It's polite to knock, you know.'

'God, sorry! I did when I came in the first time, but . . .' This had to be the nurse—but now Roger

31

was nowhere to be seen. 'Weird,' she murmured. 'Gone the same place as his bag, I guess.'

'Is something the matter with you?'

'Yeah, my head. But don't let me jump the queue. What happened to Roger?'

'The boy who was in here just now?' The nurse grinned cheerily. 'He felt faint with all this heat!'

Sara half-smiled. Was *that* why he'd seemed so shifty? 'He told me he'd hurt his ankle.'

'And now I expect he's run off to avoid embarrassment,' smiled the nurse.

'Mm,' said Sara. 'I expect so.' But she couldn't help feeling he'd been up to something.

'Well, he's freed up the couch so you can take a turn,' said the nurse. 'Feeling faint with the heat too, are we?'

'No! Feeling a wall!' said Sara. 'With my head. Very hard.'

'The wall, or the head?' chuckled the nurse, striding over to examine her. 'Hmm. That's quite a lump you have. Let's find you an ice pack.'

Sara smiled. 'I'd prefer an ice *cream*!'

'I just ate the last one,' joked the nurse as he crossed over to the small fridge-freezer in the corner.

 32

But before he could reach it, his legs seemed to skid from under him. And while he struggled to keep his balance, in the end he fell backwards just as Sam had done in the lab. Sara couldn't get clear in time, and he went crashing into her.

With a gasp and a yelp she found herself back on the floor.

'I'm so sorry!' cried the nurse. 'Are you all right?'

'I'm good,' sighed Sara. 'Just lying here thinking how bad I must have been in a former life.'

'I'd better get two ice packs,' he groaned, holding his head. 'I don't know what happened, I just sort-of slipped!'

Sara pointed to where he was sitting. 'Could that have anything to do with it?'

The nurse looked down to find his backside was parked firmly in a small puddle. 'It's cold,' he realized.

Sara frowned. 'Melted ice?' She was getting a creepy feeling of déjà vu.

'I did have some ice cubes in the icebox,' said the nurse, getting up and crossing carefully to the fridge-freezer. 'Maybe it's leaking . . .'

He opened the door. 'Funny—the ice packs

have all gone.' He reached into the back of the icebox. 'Here's the ice cube tray, anyway . . .'

He took out the tray and studied it for a moment.

Then he yelled in alarm, jumped back, and slipped in the wet patch all over again. Only this time, he hit the back of his head on the side of the sink with a convincing THUNK, and lay still.

Sara stared at him for a few seconds, speechless. Then she crouched beside him in a bit of a panic. 'Don't die!' she told him. 'You can't die on my first day!' It was OK—he was breathing. But his eyes were shut. She should check his pulse—like they did on TV. There it was—and it was, well, pulsing away. That had to be a good thing.

Then the nurse stirred, and made a groggy, whimpering sort of noise.

'It's all right,' she breathed through a flood of relief. 'You're going to be OK.'

But what had made him shout like that?

Then she saw the ice cube tray lying beside him on the floor.

The ice seemed coated with something red-black and watery.

 34

It looked like blood.

Gross!

She stood shakily and quickly ran some cold water over her wrists. Who would want to freeze blood? Aside from maybe a vampire who fancied an ice-lolly . . .

The nurse groaned again.

'Hang on, I'll go and get help,' said Sara. With her own head throbbing more than ever, she went to get the receptionist. It was shaping up to be one weird day at Freekham High.

BREAKTIME

Even with a detention looming, the breaktime bell couldn't sound soon enough for Sam.

First lessons at a new school in the middle of term were always super-dull. You didn't know what was going on. No one could be bothered to *explain* to you what was going on. And you were expected in seconds to magically soak in everything that the rest of the class had been studying for weeks.

Sam looked down at his worksheet glumly. He'd managed to answer six out of twelve questions—but three of those answers deliberately missed the point in a calculated attempt to annoy, and another two had probably missed the point by accident. Still, at least he'd definitely got his own name right.

Sara hadn't come back. He hoped she was OK and didn't hate his guts. So much for making a cool impression on his new class. He'd upset the teacher as planned—sticking to his long-established new-school strategy—but had managed to beat up three people by mistake, be unjustly accused of wetting his pants, and wind up sitting next to the biggest sucker in the school (who, of course, was *also* on a breaktime detention so there was no escape). And meanwhile, he'd given his biggest potential ally a major head injury—by now she was probably having brain surgery in the nearest casualty department.

It was all the fault of that icy water. A death trap in waiting! If Sam hadn't fallen, someone else would have—but, of course, he had got no thanks for sacrificing himself like that.

How *totally* unfair!

Stupid puddle. If Penter was really so sure the floor was dry before assembly, then someone must have sneaked in while everyone was out—and then spilled their drink or whatever. *That* person should be doing detention now, not him.

Oh, who cares, he thought. *Let it go.* The damage had been done, to both his back and his reputation. That was life—sometimes, it just sucked. Almost as hard as Ashley on his thumb.

As the rest of the class poured out of the lab for fifteen minutes of freedom before double Biology dragged them back, Sam rubbed his back and sighed. Ashley, his fellow prisoner, pulled out his thumb and offered Sam a feeble smile.

'Hey!' said Sam. 'Ashley, you were in the science block in assembly, carrying that box. Did you see anyone coming—?'

He clammed up as Penter came over, snatched their worksheets away, and handed them some sheets of lined paper.

'Right then,' said Penter. 'Your punishments. While Freekham High is a progressive school, I'm afraid my detentions have that old-fashioned touch. Mr Lamb, you will write out one hundred times, *I will not shout and cry loudly outside the assembly hall.*' He looked at Sam. 'And *you*, Mr Innocent, will write out, *I shall make a positive effort to integrate myself into my new school and show humility to my fellow pupils and respect to my teachers—two* hundred times.'

Sam nodded. 'I'm not sure I can spell all of that, but I'll give it a go.'

'You'll do more than that,' said Penter. 'These are maxims that I want you both to take to heart.' He paused. 'Now, you've got Biology in here next with Mr Kale, haven't you?'

Ashley nodded meekly.

'If you don't finish before his lesson starts, you'll continue at lunchtime. Hand the papers in to me in the staffroom.'

'Er, where *is* the staffroom, sir?' asked Sam.

Penter waved a dismissive arm. 'Ashley will show you,' he said. 'Pay attention to the route, Mr Innocent. I have no doubt you'll be retracing it many times over the coming weeks.'

With that, he marched from the room.

'It's very touching when a teacher shows that much faith in a pupil,' joked Sam.

Ashley didn't respond; just started writing his lines.

'So you were shouting and crying, huh?'

Ashley looked at Sam suspiciously. 'What do you care?'

'Just making conversation with a fellow prisoner,' said Sam. 'What happened?'

'There are these two boys in the year above, my brother's year,' sighed Ashley. 'They're always picking on me. I lost my temper and shouted at them.'

 39

Sam nodded. 'And cried, too. Loudly.'

Ashley bowed his head and sighed.

'The thumb thing, right?'

'Why shouldn't I suck my thumb!' grumped Ashley, popping the wrinkled digit back in his mouth.

Because it makes you look like a total geek? thought Sam. *Because you should have grown out of it, like, ten years ago?* But he felt a pang of sympathy for this little loser. 'Each to their own, I guess,' he said. 'Live and let suck, or whatever.'

'It's not fair,' Ashley whined. 'They tease me and beat me up, but I'm the one who gets detention off Penter!'

'Why did he send you to the science block?'

'Had to collect some old textbooks from here and take them to Horrible Hayes's charity cupboard,' said Ashley.

'Horrible Hayes?'

'The History teacher. There's some charity that takes old textbooks and recycles them into—'

'Hang on—you took those books from *this* classroom?' Sam gave him a stern look. 'Ashley, was it *you* who made that wet patch on the floor?'

 40

'No!' he protested.

'Well, what about that other guy you were with?'

Ashley shrugged. 'How should I know? He was bunking off. He was in here when I arrived.'

'Who was he, anyway?'

'Colin Cox. He's a mate of my brother.' Ashley flashed that weedy smile again. 'It was really cool—he helped me with the books! I couldn't believe it. I'd never have been able to shift them on my own.'

'Nice guy,' said Sam without much interest, picking up his pen and starting to write.

'Strange, though,' Ashley went on. 'Normally he tries to rub my face in dog muck while yelling he hates my guts.'

Sam frowned. 'Well, maybe that's why he was bunking off. He wasn't feeling himself.' He put down the pen. 'There we are. Finished.'

'Finished?' squawked Ashley. 'I've hardly started! How did you manage that?'

Sam slid his paper across the desk to Ashley. 'Just doing what he told me. And I really shall try. I only hope I don't lose count . . .'

He smiled as Ashley read the single sentence:

I shall make a positive effort to integrate myself into my new school and show respect to my fellow pupils and humility to my teachers 200 times.

Sara looked wistfully through the sickroom's window at the people hanging out and kicking back in the playground, chatting, sunning themselves, making the most of the break. And where was she? Waiting with the poorly nurse in his boiling office until help could arrive.

The receptionist had seemed completely out of her depth when trying to cope with the situation. 'But I'm a temp!' was her answer to pretty much everything. So Sara was the one who had to call for the ambulance. Sara was the one who had to fetch the receptionist some tissues when she started crying. And now Sara was the one left nursing the nurse while the receptionist sobbed down the phone to her friends.

What are you not, Sara Knot? she thought. *You are not not a soft touch.*

Still, at least she was spared the embarrassment

of standing on her own in the playground with 'Loser—no mates' stamped on her forehead. She wondered who Memphis Ball went around with. She didn't look the type to hang out with a crowd. Sara liked her—but was being friends with someone so totally strange-looking asking for trouble?

Then again, she'd had pretty much nothing but trouble ever since she'd arrived. If she asked for it, maybe it would go away.

'The ambulance is here!' cried the receptionist, in the kind of horrified tones most people would reserve for an alien invasion. She stood flapping in the doorway, her frizzy curls bouncing wildly. 'Is the nurse all right? Is he still breathing?'

'I told you, he'll be fine,' said Sara calmly, hoping she was right. 'Do the paramedics know where to find us?'

The receptionist looked at her blankly.

Sara sighed. 'OK, let's go and show them where they need to go.'

'Right. Yes. Good,' said the receptionist. 'I'm only the temp, you know, I never thought—'

'I know,' said Sara, her teeth ever-so-slightly gritted.

result  43

From the entrance hall she could see the ambulance pulling up right to the main doors, the sun's reflection dazzling from its windscreen. A seething crowd of sweaty pupils had gathered around it, chattering excitedly and heckling the bewildered ambulance workers as they emerged with a stretcher.

Sara opened the main door for them. 'He's through here,' she pointed. 'He slipped and hit the back of his head. Twice.'

The medic frowned at her.

'Don't ask,' said Sara. She wondered if she should mention the blood in the ice cube tray—but decided against it. It probably wasn't blood at all. And how much time did she want to spend tied up here, anyway?

As the paramedics pushed past her, Sara looked out of the window at the crowding people. Already some were getting bored and moving away. Some lads were starting a game of footie with a tennis ball. One of them was especially good, jumping from foot to foot like a monkey on hot coals.

It was Roger, the boy from the sickroom. He smacked the ball hard into the thigh of the player

44

opposite and his mates guffawed with laughter.

'Wonder what he's like when he's *not* feeling faint,' Sara muttered.

She checked her watch and saw it was almost time for next period: Biology, back in the lab. She'd better head off now if she was going to find it before the bell. So much science in one morning! She wouldn't be surprised if freezing blood was actually on the curriculum here.

In fact, she doubted if much could surprise her after what she'd been through already today.

And she was dead wrong.

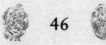

PERIODS THREE AND FOUR
BIOLOGY

Sam was sinking deeper and deeper into boredom as Ashley scrawled his lines out over the page. He cradled his head in both hands. The heat was making him drowsy, he could easily find himself drifting off to . . .

That weird, hooting alarm started up again, and Sam nearly jumped out of his skin. It was the school 'bell' again, hollering that it was time to surrender your freedom and come back inside. Assuming you'd made it out at all in the first place.

The first person in was Memphis Ball, which surprised Sam. He'd expected her to slope in last, flinging rebellion everywhere she looked. Instead she walked up to him, put her head to one side and a hand on one hip, and stared.

'Hi, Memphis,' said Sam.

She half-smiled. 'Hi, yourself.'

'You have an unusual name.'

'You noticed.' Memphis yawned. 'My parents were on holiday there when I was conceived. I'm the lucky one. My brother's name is Stoke-on-Trent.'

'You're kidding!'

'Yep,' Memphis agreed. 'So, you sitting with the thumb-chum this lesson?'

Sam glanced at Ashley who didn't look up, apparently 100 per cent absorbed in his solemn written promises to Penter. 'Do I have a choice?'

'I suppose you could always try and swap. Cabbage won't know any better,' said Memphis. Catching his blank look, she explained: 'Mr Kale, that is—our Human Biologist. Though no one's actually *sure* he's human.'

Sam grinned. 'Hey. If Sara doesn't come back, I could maybe sit with you.'

Memphis considered coolly. 'Maybe.'

'What happened to your hair, by the way?'

Her eyes flashed. 'Then again, maybe not! But since you ask . . . Well, I guess I got bored one day.'

'Bet your parents went ape, didn't they?'

'Not allowed to. If Mum gets cross it messes up her karma. She became a Buddhist last year.' Memphis mimed shaving her head. 'So when I chopped off my locks I told her it was 'cause I wanted to be just like her. She thought it was kind of sweet.'

'Buddhist, huh? They're the slapheads who like chanting and wearing funny cymbals on their fingers, right?'

'That is the most insightful summary of a religious group I ever heard,' said Memphis, keeping her face perfectly straight. 'Though you know, actually, there *are* kind of interesting ideas in Buddhism.'

'Oh yeah?' said Sam without much enthusiasm. Was she only being friendly so she could try to convert him?

He was saved by Sara peering around the doorway.

'Aha,' said Memphis, green eyes sparkling like the sun on the sea. 'If you're Yang, here comes Yin.'

Sam frowned. 'Huh? Is that more Buddhist stuff?'

'Chinese.'

'The only Chinese I know comes in foil boxes with special fried rice.'

But the joke was lost on Memphis, who was already walking over to meet Sara. Sam tagged along after her.

'How're you feeling, Sara?' he called, getting in first.

'Not great.' She grimaced at him before turning to Memphis. 'You won't believe what's been happening.'

'Weird stuff, right?' said Memphis knowingly. 'Anything to do with that ambulance?'

Sam frowned. 'Ambulance?'

'Yeah, it came for the nurse,' said Sara. 'He'd barely taken one look at me when he fell over.'

Memphis didn't seem surprised. 'So *you* called for the ambulance, right?'

'Not till he fell the second time. He went to get me an ice pack, banged his head and lights out.'

Sam raised an eyebrow. 'Are you used to having guys falling at your feet?'

Sara raised a fist. 'Only when I deck them. And I've got a very sore head, thanks to you, so don't mess.'

 49

'Now, now,' said Memphis, stepping between them while returning pupils filed into the room around them. 'What made him fall, Sara?'

'There was some water on the floor.' Sara glanced at Sam. 'Icy water.'

'Icy water?' Sam's eyes lit up. 'You sure?'

'Uh-huh.'

'Kind of a weird coincidence, isn't it?' said Memphis.

'I've been talking to the thumb-chum—' Sam jerked a thumb behind him at Ashley— 'Remember we saw him lugging that big box out of the science block?'

Sara nodded. 'With another guy.'

'Right—Colin Cox, his name is. And it turns out that the box was being kept in this room. But get this . . .' Sam paused impressively. 'That other guy was *already here* when Ashley came to get it!'

'Whoop-de-doo,' said Sara. 'So what?'

'Well,' said Sam, his feelings slightly hurt. 'If Ashley didn't spill the water, and Penter said the floor was dry, then most likely it was Colin Cox! I bet you he went to the sickroom afterwards and did it again. He's probably spilling ice cubes all over the school—just so poor saps like me get into trouble.'

Memphis wrinkled her long nose. 'Poor ickle diddums.'

'Well, if it was him, I didn't see him,' said Sara. 'There *was* a guy already in there, but he didn't stick around long once I turned up. Didn't want to admit he'd fainted.' She paused. 'It's weird, I felt like maybe he was up to something. And I'm sure I've seen him somewhere before . . .'

'Maybe in the hall this morning, when you were signing in,' Sam suggested.

Sara shrugged. 'Probably. Anyway, the nurse said loads of people had come in, dropping in the heat. Maybe your Colin Cox was one of them.'

Memphis tugged at her shirt collar. 'It's so hot today, I'm surprised the water didn't just sizzle away the second it spilled.'

'Anyway, never mind the water—get this.' She paused while both Sam and Memphis leaned in. 'I found some red stuff in the ice tray. It may have been *blood*!'

'Blood?' Memphis whispered. 'Wow! That is *totally* creepy!'

 51

'Maybe the nurse keeps blood here for . . .' Sam racked his brains. 'I dunno. Emergency transfusions or something?'

'Sure,' said Sara. 'And they store it right next to the school operating theatre.'

'Operating theatre?' boomed a voice behind them. 'Stay calm! You're only dissecting rats today!'

Sam turned to see a cheery man with a seriously dimpled chin and a mop of curly black hair striding up to them.

'Cabbage Kale,' hissed Memphis. 'Enjoy.' She slunk off to her seat at the back of the room.

'So, you're the two new kids on the block, eh?' said Kale. 'Sam and Sara, isn't it?'

'Yup,' said Sam.

'Well, I won't expect you to pick up everything straight away,' he said, eyes darting between the two of them. 'I'll give you ten minutes! How about that?' He grinned, and this time his whole head swung between them like a fat round pendulum as he searched for a reaction. 'I'm joking!' he told them. 'Obviously!'

Sam and Sara managed weak smiles.

'I'll give you *twenty* minutes!' Kale added, and

snorted with amusement. 'No, that was a joke too!'

'Gotcha,' said Sam, forcing a smile. He was too taken with this latest turn in the ice-water mystery to bother baiting another teacher. 'Good one, sir.'

'I may be a teacher but I'm a bit crazy with it,' chuckled Kale.

Aren't they all, thought Sam.

'Now, got yourselves somewhere to sit?'

Sara nodded. 'I'm next to Memphis.'

'Technically I do,' Sam began, 'but I was thinking maybe I—'

'You've been put next to Ashley, eh, Sam? Well, good, good.' Kale beamed at them both. 'Off you go, then.'

Choice. Sam heard several sniggers as he sat back down beside Ashley, still bent almost double over his lines, oblivious to all. Then he realized his own pieces of paper were missing. Not just his jokey lines, but the notes he'd made during first lesson.

He looked up sharply. The mousy-looking girl opposite was staring vacantly into space. She looked as if she'd think twice about blinking, let

 53

alone taking someone's property. Then the obvious answer presented itself bluntly: Ruth Cook was holding the papers and smirking unpleasantly.

'Very funny,' she sneered, tapping a finger against the single sentence he'd written for Penter. 'So clever, aren't you?'

Sam briefly considered this. 'Compared to you, maybe,' he concluded.

'If you mess with me, you're a bigger sucker than *he* is,' she muttered, glaring at Ashley. So saying, she snatched *his* paper from his greasy grip. He gave a plaintive 'Eep!' of alarm and stuck his thumb back in his gob.

Sam looked around to see where Kale was, in case he'd noticed. But the burly man was on all fours, peering into the cupboard beside the fume cabinet. The sound of chatter was slowly rising around the classroom. He noticed that Sara and Memphis were talking quite animatedly, and wished he could hear more about what had happened in the sickroom.

Instead, he had this dreary hard girl to contend with. Sam wasn't much of a fighter, but there were usually other ways to win battles. Ruth was folding Sam's pieces of paper together with Ashley's to make some kind of paper aeroplane.

'Know what they call me?' she challenged.

'Uh, Ruth?'

'Ruthless.'

'Because you don't have much up top?'

'*What?*'

'Oh, sorry—*Ruthless*! I thought you said "Roofless".'

'Ha, ha,' she said, aiming her (actually very finely-crafted, Sam had to admit) paper aeroplane at the bin by the teacher's desk. 'Well, you know where *this* lot is going.'

Ashley mumbled some kind of pitiful plea for her to stop, but it was too muffled by the thumb in his mouth.

Then, at the last possible moment, Cabbage Kale supplied a stay of execution.

'Shut up, you lot!' he said crossly, his cheerful demeanour gone, both white cheeks consumed by red fluster. 'As you know, we were supposed to be dissecting rats today. But the rats I ordered have not arrived.'

('Can you blame them?' murmured Memphis.)

'They were supposed to have been delivered

 55

this morning,' Kale informed them. 'I'd better check with reception. See what's happened to them.'

(*Good luck getting anything out of her*, thought Sara.)

'Stay here and stay quiet,' said Kale. 'I won't be long . . .' He paused, glancing around the class, a smile sneaking on to his face despite himself. 'I'll be my *usual height*!'

You could have heard the tumbleweeds blowing around the classroom. Kale tried his best not to look crestfallen. 'Yes, well. I did tell you to stay quiet, didn't I?'

A millisecond after he walked out of the lab, the class erupted back into noisy chatter. Ruth glared at Sam threateningly. With Kale out of the way, she was free to do something he might regret. Dazzling her with wit wasn't working— perhaps a change in tactics was in order.

'Cabbage can't help you now, losers,' said Ruth, raising her right arm with the plane held high. She threw with a champion dart player's precision. It sailed over and landed nose first in the bin, a direct hit.

'You know, I was prepared to loathe you at

first sight,' Sam admitted. 'But that was actually pretty cool.'

Ruth narrowed her eyes, suspicious.

'I mean it!' he protested. 'Not just any plane, either, was it? Looked like a stealth bomber or something.'

Ruth shrugged, but looked secretly pleased. 'Harrier jump-jet.'

'A Harrier, huh?'

'My brother taught me how to make them,' she went on. 'He knows everything about them. He's a mechanic.'

'And he works on planes?'

'Nah. But he did try to steal one once.'

'Cool,' said Sam through a big fake grin. 'Well, a home-made Harrier. This I have to see at close range.' He slipped from his stool and went over to the bin to retrieve the plane.

But as he removed it from the bin, he frowned.

The nose of the paper plane was soggy. It was tinged a watery red.

He picked out a crumpled piece of paper beneath the plane. It was sodden and pink as well. There was water in this bin—cold, icy water.

And just a trace of . . .

No, it couldn't be.

Blood?

'Ugh!' muttered Sam, shaking his fingers. Sara thought she had found blood in the melted ice tray. Now he'd found some here in the watery bin. What was going on? That puddle he'd slipped in . . . Had it been formed when something cold and wet and gross was fished out of the bin?

Or, had this cold, wet, gross something been taken from somewhere else and thrown *into* the bin?

In which case it would still be here, hidden by soaked, stained rubbish . . .

As if his arm had a will of its own, Sam found himself reaching down into the bin once again . . .

'Oi!' complained Ruthless noisily. 'Stop nobbing about and get back here with that plane! I'll show you how it's done if you want.'

Sam jumped and swore as he was jarred back to reality. He opened his mouth, about to tell her—tell the whole class—what he'd seen.

And froze.

The new kid. On his first day. Finds something nasty and weird in the bin. Yeah, just happens to stumble across it. Didn't secretly put it there himself because he's some mad FREAK trying to seem interesting, oh no. No way.

'What's up with you?' she demanded.

'Nothing,' he said, forcing a smile. He'd tell Sara and Memphis before he told anyone. But he had to find out what was in that bin . . .

'Do you want to know how it's done or not!' Ruth said, scowling.

'That'd be great,' he sighed. If he wanted to avoid his *own* blood spilling around here, he guessed he'd better go stroke Ruth's ego a little more. He handed her the soggy paper.

'Give me my lines back,' said Ashley, 'please!' Ruth ignored him. 'It's wet,' she said.

'Yeah, there was . . . a cup of water in the bin or something,' said Sam. 'And some, uh, red paint.'

'Weird,' said Ruth.

You don't know the half of it, thought Sam. 'Tell you what, never mind the Harrier. Let's unfold it and leave it to dry, and you can show me another one from scratch.' He took the soggy

59

plane back from her and subtly passed it to the grateful Ashley. 'You like planes, huh, Ruth?'

'Yeah. You know the Harrier can do 730 miles per hour?'

'Wow!' *Or over a thousand if it saw you coming after it.* 'So, do you make these things to any other designs?'

'Well . . .' The plan was working: Ruth seemed chuffed at the sudden interest. 'B2 stealth bomber?'

'Show me, show me, show me.'

Sara tutted and shook her head. She'd been watching Sam.

'What is that boy like?' she grumped to Memphis. 'Fishing around in the bin, mucking about with paper aeroplanes—and now cosying up with *Ruth Cook*!'

'If you have to mix with her, she makes a better friend than an enemy,' Memphis advised.

'Why so bothered?' someone said behind her. 'Is he your boyfriend or something?'

Sara recognized the low, cultured voice—it was the boy who'd called out when Penter had

 60

welcomed them to the school, the comedian. She looked up in surprise to see a tall, slim boy looking at her expectantly. He had clear, slightly critical blue eyes, a long nose, and an untidy thatch of brown hair. Sara felt herself flush; he was kind of cute.

'Sam Innocent is not my boyfriend!' protested Sara. 'I hardly know him.'

''K, keep your hair on. Ever so long, isn't it? Your hair, I mean.' The boy grinned. 'You have good bone structure, by the way.'

Sara blinked and swept her hair over her shoulder on reflex. 'You're a bit random, aren't you?'

'I'm a film director,' he said grandly. 'I notice such things in my potential leading ladies.'

'Sara, meet Fido Tennant,' said Memphis.

'Fido?' echoed Sara.

'This is what they call me,' admitted Fido. 'Because I work like a hound in my pursuit of the good life.'

'As long as it's not because you bite the postman and pee up lamp-posts. What's your real name?'

'Dorian.'

'We'll stick to Fido,' Sara decided. 'So. You direct films?'

'Almost,' Fido confessed. 'I have a camcorder. I'm working on a screenplay.' He leaned forward confidently. 'And I'm always looking for fresh talent.'

'Stay on your leash, Fido.' Sara smiled tightly. 'You'd do better looking for fresh chat-up lines.'

Fido smiled back. 'As soon as I saw you I knew we'd get on famously.'

'I don't want to be famous,' said Sara, looking up at him from under her lashes. 'Sorry.'

'You give good dialogue, I like that,' said Fido, turning to go again, a little glow of red warming his cheeks. 'You know, Sara, this could be the beginning of a beautiful friendship!'

'He seems kind of cool,' Sara observed.

'He got nicknamed Fido years back for being barking mad,' said Memphis. 'Obsessed with making movies. But you're right. He *is* kind of cool.'

'We approve?'

Memphis smiled cannily. 'We approve. And what about Sam?'

'Cocky. Show off.' Sara paused. 'But has potential.'

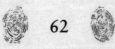

62

Memphis nodded and fixed her with those sea-green eyes. 'He has *weird* potential . . .'

While Ruth deftly turned and folded paper, Sam was feeling jittery. Could that *really* be blood in the bin-water?

Part of him wanted to look again.

Another part thought he should leave well alone, terrified of what he might find inside. A big, sticky leech preserved in ice? Some rare, icy, bloodsucking creature escaped from somewhere?

He had to find out. But yet another part of him knew that if he started rummaging in bins, people would think that *he'd* escaped from somewhere.

No, it was better to leave it to fate. Wait for Ruth to finish her next plane. If it hit the bin like its predecessor, he'd fish it back out like before. And maybe then he'd find—

'There,' said Ruth proudly. 'What d'ya think?' She'd gone from savage animal to pussycat in as much time as she took to build a B2 bomber from lined A4.

'I think it's awesome,' said Sam. 'Will she fly the same as the last one?'

'Better,' said Ruth. She smiled at him. 'Give me a target, I'll have their eye out with this. No problem.'

'Nice thought, but how about you try dive-bombing the bin again?' Sam took a deep breath. 'Hey, tell you what—I'll soak up some of that water first, so it's safe to land.'

'Don't bother,' said Ruth, grabbing hold of Mousy by her shirtsleeve. The girl's vacant expression turned to one of panic. 'We'll send Minger Harris to do it.'

'No!' Sam almost shouted.

Ruth screwed up her face. 'Er? Why not? It's all she's good for.'

'Um, because . . .' Sam's mind raced. If that *was* blood in the bin—and if whatever was bleeding was still inside—poor little Mousy would go to pieces. Besides, this was Sam's private discovery, and until he knew more about it, no one else would.

'I'm waiting,' said Ruth. 'Why *not*?'

Sam's mind was a blank. 'Well, because . . .'

Ruth almost snarled: 'Because you like her better than me?'

'Uh . . .' Sam faltered. Comparing the two was like comparing a punch to the face with a kick in the stomach—you'd prefer to avoid either if you could help it. But if he didn't come up with a good reason soon, Ruthless Cook would no doubt be delivering both those blows and more besides.

With perfect timing, the classroom door opened and Cabbage Kale returned with a face like thunder.

'Because *he's* back,' Sam finished lamely, sliding round the table back to his seat. 'Guess the show's over.'

Mousy Minger Harris looked at him as if he was her hero. Ashley sucked his thumb and clutched his lines to his chest as though they were love letters. And Ruth huffily hurled her B2 bomber at Sam and—with deadly accuracy—caught him right in the eye.

'Told you!' Ruth gloated. 'No problem!'

'That's enough, all of you,' said Kale crossly, and the classroom noise subsided. 'Seems there's been some mix up and my rats have gone astray. They should have been here first thing, but . . .' He shook his head and gave up, apparently

65

realizing the class didn't exactly mind that rat gizzards were off today's biological menu. He clapped his hands together and forced a brighter expression. 'Oh well! We'll just have to look at some photographs of cut-up rats instead! I've got some laminated ones somewhere . . .'

The class swapped 'whoopee' looks with each other—except Sam, whose eye was watering too badly. In any case, his mind was elsewhere. Missing rats . . . and cold, bloody water in a bin. Maybe the rats had been delivered to the lab all right—but they'd escaped. Maybe Colin Cox had set them free—he'd come here alone this morning on a rescue mission. *Or*, maybe he'd seen one escaping, grabbed it and there had been a struggle—boy versus rat. He drowned the rat in icy water, and then poured the poor squashed rodent into the bin. But then what about the blood in the icebox in the sickroom? Had another rat been injured, and Roger gone to the sickroom to try and help it? When that didn't work, had he shoved the rat in the icebox to keep it fresh?

He had to admit, his theory didn't sound likely. But then he hadn't expected to be hit in the eye by a B2 bomber either. Now he'd pooh-poohed Ruth's plans, she was back to giving him dirty looks. But Minger Harris was looking shyly in his direction.

Kale passed out the gruesome laminated rat studies. Sam took a good look at the pictures, bracing himself. Later on, he might be seeing rat guts for real.

BREATHER

With the rest of the lesson spent trawling through a typical rodent's lower intestine, Sam felt he was getting a pretty good grounding for his impending mission. When the end-of-lesson bell finally rang, a sense of destiny overcame him.

'Are we out of time? RATS!' chortled Kale, taking back his picture collection of well-ventilated rats. 'Your homework is to describe the complete path of a piece of cheese through the rat's digestive system, fully explaining everything that happens to it along the way.'

'What's to explain?' wondered Sam aloud. 'It goes in one end, it comes out the other.' Then again, maybe he could just cut open the binned rat and sellotape it into his exercise book, get extra credits . . .

'You're a big disappointment, Innocent,' said

Ruth gruffly. 'I thought you were going to be a laugh.'

'I am!' he protested. 'Isn't it *plane* to see?'

She snorted and stalked out. Ashley and Minger Harris followed on nervously some distance away.

'Hell hath no fury like a woman scorned,' said Sara, she and Memphis walking over to join him.

'Never mind that.' Sam checked Cabbage Kale was leaving the room, and spoke to them urgently. 'That bin! I reckon there's something inside it.'

'There is,' said Sara gravely.

'What?'

'Rubbish.' She cracked up into slightly horsy laughter, and Memphis joined in.

'I'm serious,' Sam hissed. 'Something horrid is in there. Something totally way-out gross. Something dead—or wounded, I guess. Or—'

'What are you on about?' asked Memphis.

'There's bloody water in the bin!'

'No way!' said Sara, looking freaked out.

'I reckon it could be one of the missing rats!' said Sam. 'So let's find out.'

'We don't have long,' Memphis told them. 'Breather's only five minutes.'

The three of them crossed to the bin and peered inside. The water lined its base.

'Must have been a fair bit of ice in there,' breathed Memphis.

'The water's not cold any more,' Sam reported, reaching in past the soggy paper and feeling gingerly around. 'This heat must have melted the ice double-quick.'

'What am I doing here?' wondered Sara. 'Do I really want to see a dead rat?'

Sam bit his lip. 'I've found something.'

Memphis and Sara looked at him expectantly. 'Well?'

He frowned. 'It's a bit small to be a rat . . .' The thing felt cold, thin, and slightly squashy as his fingers closed around it. He pulled it out and opened his palm.

Sam, Sara, and Memphis found themselves looking at a human finger.

'AUUGGGHHHHHHH!' yelled Sam, recoiling with shock and flinging it in the air. Sara and Memphis yelled with him and scattered.

Sam fell over backwards, eyes wide and staring

as the finger fell back down to earth. It bounced once on the gleaming tiles, then lay there, skinny and still and slug-like.

Sam thought he might throw up. It was a woman's finger by the look of it. He rushed to one of the sinks to wash his sticky hand.

'Gross me out the door!' groaned Sara. 'Where did *that* come from?'

Memphis crawled out from under the table, fascination on her face. 'I don't know,' she murmured. 'But look at the end.'

Sara clutched her stomach. 'Should I be impressed with her manicure?'

'Other end. It's been cut cleanly.'

Sam dried his hand on his trouser leg, swallowed down the sick feeling, and took a closer look. Memphis was right.

'So, what, it was cut with a sharp knife?' he ventured.

'Like a surgeon would use?' wondered Sara. 'Ugh. I wish it *had* been a rat now.'

'Maybe someone's been hurt,' said Sam.

'It doesn't exactly look fresh, does it?' Memphis shuddered. 'I reckon that thing's been knocking about for ages. The ice was keeping it fresh.'

 71

'Good point.'

'Thanks.'

Sam smiled at her. 'I was talking to the finger!'

'Ho, ho,' said Memphis. 'Question is, are there any more of them in that bin?'

'Someone else's turn to check,' said Sam.

Sara looked at him. 'Don't think so.'

'Here.' Memphis passed him a thirty centimetre ruler from her bag. 'You can use this.'

'I'm touched,' he said. Taking a deep breath, he held it while he carefully poked about. After a few tense moments, he shook his head. 'No more of them.'

'Like, how totally disappointing,' joked Sara.

'Hey, wait a minute!' said Sam. 'That receptionist! She only had one hand.'

Sara gave him a doubtful look. 'So what, you think it dropped off and broke, and we've just found one of the pieces?'

'Mrs Willow lost her hand over a year ago now,' Memphis told them. 'A bizarre lawn-mowing accident. She was out gardening, right—'

'She had green fingers,' said Sam solemnly.

'—and the lawnmower was playing up so she was fiddling with the cable, see, when—'

'OK, we get the picture,' said Sara quickly. 'Thing is—what are we going to do with that thing?'

'Dump it back in the bin where we found it?' Sam suggested.

'We have to tell a teacher,' said Sara.

'Do we?' wondered Memphis.

'Of course we do!'

Memphis looked at her. 'What, and tell them we happened to find a severed human finger while poking about the bins in the science block?'

Sam sighed. 'They'll think it's one of my stunts.'

'Just your luck,' said Sara. 'You give some cheek, and get a finger.'

He winced. 'And I think I've had enough hassle for one day.'

'I agree with Sam,' said Memphis. 'It's not like we're handing in a purse or something—they'll think we *all* had something to do with it. Especially if Penter gets to hear of it.'

'But . . .' Sara frowned. 'Someone . . . someone may be looking for it.'

There was a wicked glint in Memphis's eye. 'You think maybe Mrs Willow kept her fingers as souvenirs?'

'It's not funny!' complained Sara.

'But it is very, *very* weird.' Memphis seemed half-excited, half-nervous. 'I just *knew* something freaky would be going down around here, the minute I found out about you two.'

Sara raised her eyebrows. 'Thanks!'

'What are you on about?' Sam asked.

'First things first. Let's put the finger back in the bin and get out of here before the next class come in.'

Sam tore some blank pages from his Biology book and used them to scoop up the finger. It hit the bin with a soft plopping noise, and he scattered the papers over the top. 'There. It should stay well hidden now.'

'What if someone finds it?' asked Sara.

'I'd say we'd probably hear them all the way from the English block,' said Memphis.

'At least then it's not our problem any more,' Sam pointed out. 'Let someone else worry about it.'

'I'd say someone already is,' said Sara quietly. 'I reckon they may have found another one. The blood in the icebox in the sickroom—remember?'

Sam drew a sharp breath. 'You think there's a finger ice-pop in there?'

Sara shrugged and headed for the door. 'Let's just get out of here. Suddenly, double English is sounding like deep joy.'

Sara's legs were wobbling as they left the science block and its grisly secret behind them. All around them, guys and girls were shuffling, scuffling, yelling, and shoving their way to their next lessons like they would in any school. It all seemed gorgeously normal. What had just happened in Penter's form room didn't seem possible. Had she knocked herself on the head harder than she'd thought? Was she dreaming?

She pinched herself but the world around her stayed just as real and hot and humid as ever.

'I don't believe today could get any stranger,' she said, shaking her aching head wearily.

'Things started off kind of odd, didn't they?' said Sam thoughtfully, still wiping his hand obsessively against his trouser leg. 'You and me both arriving here, having so much in common—'

Sara nodded. 'And they just got weirder and weirder.'

'Totally,' Memphis agreed breezily. Sara couldn't believe how laid back she was being. 'And I reckon it's down to you two. Sam and Sara. *Samsara*.'

Sam and Sara both looked at her. 'Huh?' they chorused.

'It's a Buddhist word. I've heard my mum talk about it with her friends. It means . . . well, it's sort of like reincarnation based on what you did in the past. You know?'

'No,' said Sam.

'You've lost me,' agreed Sara.

'Look, we all call Freekham High the madhouse,' said Memphis patiently, steering them through the crowded corridors. 'Not just because all the teachers drive you crazy, but because it's built on the site of a place for lunatics that burnt to the ground. And *that* place was built on the site of an old government building— which was struck by lightning and blown to pieces.'

'Kind of a lucky place then,' said Sara with a shudder.

'But do you get the link?' asked Memphis.

Sam always seemed ready to hazard a guess. 'All politicians are loonies. All teachers are loonies. And obviously, all loonies are loonies.'

Memphis gave him a look. 'What I was trying to get at is that although the world seems to change, really it stays the same. That's what samsara is all about—the same stuff coming round again and again.'

'Maybe you should check into a *real* madhouse,' said Sam.

Memphis rolled her eyes. 'Look. These are the facts. You both came into the world at exactly the same time on the freakiest day in the calendar. And you both came *here* at exactly the same time, to a place where so many freaky things have happened throughout history, it's even *named* Freekham. And the moment you do, freaky stuff starts happening again.'

Sam and Sara swapped doubtful looks.

'I mean, just put your surnames together,' Memphis went on. 'Knot plus Innocent equals *not innocent*! Who knows? Maybe you were so freaky in a past life, you have to go through even freakier stuff in *this* one.'

'Sounds pretty far-fetched to me,' said Sara.

'And me,' Sam agreed.

'And finding a severed finger in a bin isn't?' Memphis's gangly body suddenly shook with laughter. 'Maybe it *is* just coincidence. Who cares? Far-fetched is fun! Life's cooler that way.'

'If only it *was* cooler,' said Sara, pulling at her shirt collar.

A few steps later, Memphis gestured to a doorway. 'Anyway. This is us. English in Miss Bedfellow's room. She's kind of cool—for one of *them*.'

Even as she spoke, the bell rang for the end of breather.

'I'm not going in,' Sam announced. 'Stuff to do.'

Sara frowned. 'You're bunking off?'

'I feel really faint,' he said dramatically, pushing a hand through his wet black spikes of hair. 'I think I'd better go to the sickroom.'

'Duh,' said Sara. 'The nurse isn't there, he's in hospital, remember?'

'Shame,' said Sam with a crafty smile. 'Guess I'll just have to poke around his freezer for stray severed fingers by myself, won't I?'

 78

'Sam, leave it, can't you?' Sara complained. 'Like you said, don't you reckon you've had enough hassle today?'

'I don't like unsolved mysteries,' said Sam. 'Besides, you heard what the girl said . . .' He grinned and gave her a spooky stare. 'It's our destiny! Now, come on, Mystic Memphis, how about you point me in the right direction? Your own finger will do.'

Memphis smiled. 'Turn left at the end of the corridor, then turn right and left again. Keep going and you can't miss it.'

'Thanks,' said Sam. 'If anyone asks after me, tell them I'm sick.'

'You *are* sick,' Sara told him. 'But watch out for yourself, OK?'

He nodded and smiled. Then he turned and made off through the thinning crowds in the direction of the school office.

Periods Five and Six

English

Sara sighed. It was still so hot, and her head was still stinging. The thought of the finger was still vivid in her mind. But while she wished she could blot out the sight of the dodgy digit, there was Sam hot on the trail of another one.

Sara supposed it proved that there were *some* differences between the two of them. She didn't want to add any more fuel to Memphis's freaky fire.

'You want to sit with me again?' asked Memphis. 'Or have I scared you off?'

Sara forced a smile, shook her head as Memphis led her across the classroom to a desk in the back row at the far corner of the room. 'Have you been sitting alone in every lesson?'

'I've been beating people off with sticks wanting to share my company,' Memphis joked. 'Most people don't know how to take me. So they ignore me. That's cool. It means I can watch 'em from a distance. I love just watching stuff, you know?'

Sara didn't really, but nodded anyway.

'You, on the other hand . . .' Memphis sat down. 'I'm guessing that watching's not enough. You get involved whenever you can. Sometimes despite yourself, right?'

Sara thought back to the events of breaktime. 'I guess.'

'Soft touch.' Memphis was looking past her, out through the classroom door. 'I think we're about to see just *how* soft.'

Sara turned to see someone had come up behind Ashley and grabbed hold of him. It was the tall, hook-nosed boy who'd been so rude to her outside the science block.

'Colin Cox,' said Memphis. 'Sam should have stuck around. Here's his chief suspect.'

'Get off, Colin,' said Ashley, struggling helplessly.

'Make me, loser,' grinned Colin.

Ashley shut his eyes and sucked on his thumb.

Then another guy muscled in. He had brown hair, a red face, and wide, shifty eyes. It was Roger, the faker from the sickroom—and

81

suddenly Sara knew why she'd thought she recognized him.

Roger looked kind of like Ashley.

'Memphis,' hissed Sara. 'That's the boy I was telling you about. Roger the dodger!'

'Roger Lamb!' exclaimed Memphis. 'Ashley's big brother.'

Now Sara understood the resemblance. 'And in the nick of time, too, by the look of things.'

'Oi, Colin, get out of it,' said Roger, pushing him aside and slipping his arm around Ashley. He smiled. 'You can't pick on him—that's *my* job!'

With a laugh, he shoved Ashley into the classroom, laughing as his brother went sprawling into a desk and dropped his bag.

'Try to stay out of trouble, sucker,' said Roger. Then he slouched away. Colin threw a sour look at his back, then stormed off in the other direction.

'There's brotherly love for you,' said Sara.

'Got him out of trouble, though,' Memphis pointed out. 'Without seeming like he was soft and sappy.'

Sara nodded. 'I guess.'

Ashley was picking himself up amid sniggers and stares. His cheeks were bright red, and his thumb went straight back in his mouth.

'Are you all right?' called Sara, rising from her place to give him a hand.

Ashley ignored her, picking up his bag and fiddling with the strap as if she wasn't there.

'Ha! Ha! Look at the thumb-chum's back!' Ruth Cook guffawed.

Suddenly the dozy-looking ginger kid came up behind Ashley and kicked him in the bum. Ruth roared with laughter. Ashley staggered forwards a few steps, but kept walking, looking dead ahead—as though if he didn't react, nothing could hurt him.

'Only doing as I'm told!' grinned the ginger kid.

Sara felt a small shock of anger. She didn't like dweebs, but bullies were just pathetic—and the people who cheered them on were probably worse. She realized that between ambulances and snipped fingers, she hadn't had much time to get to know her classmates. On this kind of evidence, she hadn't been missing much.

 83

Fido Tennant strolled into the room, taking in the situation in a few swift, sharp glances. 'Sort your life out, Ashley,' he said wearily, 'someone's stuck a sign on your back.'

Ashley presented his back to Sara now as he took his place at the desk in front. A piece of paper had been taped there. It said, KICK MY BUTT in silver ink capitals with a black marker outline. She plucked it off him for a closer inspection.

'New girl's got the hots for Ashley,' jeered Ruth Cook, to a few half-hearted sniggers.

'Ha, ha,' said Sara. It wasn't the greatest comeback in the world, but then wit was probably wasted on Ruth Cook.

Ashley didn't turn round, didn't thank her, he didn't respond at all. Just acted as if nothing was happening.

'I don't get him,' muttered Sara, sitting down.

Memphis looked lazily at her with big cat eyes. 'He used to get angry when people picked on him. They just laughed.' She shrugged. 'Then he tried joking with them, putting himself down. That didn't work either. So now he just pretends they're not there. Kind of sad, huh?'

Sara gave her a pointed look. 'And you're just a watcher—so, of course, you can't get involved?'

'If he stopped sucking his thumb at school, he'd have it a lot easier,' Memphis remarked. 'Sometimes people have to help themselves.'

'I guess.' Sara looked down at the KICK MY BUTT sign. She was about to screw it up when something caught her attention. There was a line of official-looking type in the top left corner. Part of it had been obliterated by the silver ink but she could still read:

CAUTION—IF SEAL TAMPERED WITH

The paper was slightly rumpled, too, as if it had got wet and then dried out again. There was type on it, too, beneath the obliterating silver letters; small bleary type that had run where water had got to it.

'What is it?' asked Memphis.

'Not sure,' muttered Sara, peering closely at the paper. 'I think it's a delivery note. You know, the kind you get with parcels.' She put it down. 'Probably nothing.'

Memphis leaned in for a look. 'I wonder why it warned about tampering with the seal?'

'Maybe it was addressed to a fur trapper. If you tamper with a seal . . .'

'You're starting to sound like Sam.'

'Oh, *thanks*.'

Sara reached into her bag, pulled out her frameless reading specs and perched them on her nose. 'Look. I think that bit says, *store below minus thirty* . . .'

'Kind of low,' said Memphis, leaning in to look at the paper herself. 'In fact that's incredibly cold. Colder than any normal freezer gets, isn't it?'

Sara shrugged. The rest of the words she could see were badly blurred. 'What do you think that bit says?'

Memphis squinted. 'Index?'

'And I think that bit says "digit" or "digits" . . .'

'So it's an index of digits and not to be tampered with?'

'Or maybe . . .' Sara turned to Memphis with a creepy, fizzing feeling in her guts. 'They're talking about index *fingers*.'

'And other digits?' Memphis pulled a scandalized face. 'Oh my God! A package of fingers!'

Sara took off her glasses. 'That warning about

 86

tampering with the seal . . . It would mean the contents wouldn't be sterile!' She leaned forward and tapped Ashley on the shoulder. 'Hey! Who stuck this to your back? Was it Colin Cox?'

Ashley didn't turn around or respond. She tried again, but he just sat there.

'You won't get anything out of him,' said Memphis.

'Whoever had this bit of paper might have the rest of the parcel!' hissed Sara. 'But who would be sending a package of fingers in the post, anyway? And why?'

'Miss Bedfellow,' said Memphis.

Sara frowned. 'You reckon a *teacher* sent—?'

'No—Miss Bedfellow's *here*!'

Sara turned round to find a confident, sassy-looking woman in a tasteful grey business suit stride into the room. Her sharp nose was held high in the air, leading the way, and long frizzy dark curls streamed out behind her.

'Right, you lot, shut up,' Miss Bedfellow said casually, and the class fell silent. Her blue eyes zeroed in on Sara. 'New girl. Sara Knot, right?'

'Right,' said Sara.

'Nice to meet you,' she said, and actually

seemed to mean it. She looked around the classroom. 'What about the new boy—Innocent Sam?'

Sara swapped a brief look with Memphis. 'He's not feeling very well, miss. He's gone to see the nurse.'

'Something in his eye,' sniggered Ruth quietly.

'How unfortunate, getting behind already on his first day,' said Miss Bedfellow. 'Still, I'm sure when he's back he'll be knuckling down.'

Knuckling down . . . Sara looked at the delivery note and bit her lip. *Maybe sooner than you think*, she thought.

Sam found the sickroom was locked. The new receptionist was clearly more capable than Sara had thought. Typical girl that Sara, he decided. Exaggerating reality to make herself look good . . .

Mind you, it was no exaggeration to say that she *did* look good. There were worse people he could have been chosen by fate to be paired with at Freekham High. He shook his head. What was Memphis like? She was seriously weird . . . But kind of fun.

Shaking his head, Sam walked through the humid, empty entrance hall to check on the receptionist now. There she was, crouched over the phone with her back to the counter, frizzy hair half-standing on end as she gassed to whoever was on the other end.

'Well, I mean, you wouldn't believe the morning I've had, honey,' she was saying. 'I mean, I'm only a temp and they expect me to cope all by myself . . .'

Suddenly, Sam's magpie eyes spied a gleaming set of chrome keys resting on the table just the other side of the counter. He reached in automatically to pick them up . . .

But as if she had eyes hidden somewhere in that mad frizz of curls, the temp abruptly spun round in her swivel chair. Sam ducked out of sight and held his breath.

'. . . Well, I know I should complain, but who to? The head's some old stiff with scary eyes . . .'

Sam breathed a sigh of relief. She couldn't have seen him. He peeped over the counter top and saw she was back facing away from him again. He reached in and stealthily took the keys, then crept away before she or anyone else could catch him.

'One of these must open the sickroom,' Sam muttered, trying to find likely candidates. After three false attempts he hit the jackpot. The key turned, the door pushed open, and he was in.

Glancing around, he saw the ice cube tray on the sun-soaked desk. Its contents were completely melted now, and there was a crimson stain to them. Sam remembered from his cleaning up a childhood of scraped knees that blood went a long way in water. It wouldn't have taken much to cause this dark colour. Just a few stray drops from a melting finger . . .

With a shudder, Sam checked the small fridge and its icebox. A few telltale spots of blood had darkened the crunchy ice crystals. Apart from them, the icebox was empty, and only some small bottles of water were stacked up in the fridge.

'Ice packs,' muttered Sam, helping himself to one of the bottles. 'Sara said the nurse went to get some ice packs . . . so where are they?' He took a cooling swig of water. Whoever had first chanced upon that finger in Penter's room and dumped it in the bin—the most likely candidate being Colin Cox—they had almost certainly brought another one here. That would explain the blood and icy water . . . And if there were no ice packs, perhaps Colin had pinched them to keep the finger fresh in this horrible heat.

'Sherlock Holmes, you're history,' said Sam with satisfaction. But he knew that he had barely solved the basics of this case. Colin Cox was one sick puppy. What was he up to?

Draining his drink, Sam checked the coast was clear and sneaked out of the sickroom, locking the door behind him. He knew he had to get the keys back to the office before they were missed.

As he approached the school office he heard the bass drawl of Cabbage Kale talking to the receptionist. Carefully, he crept closer, peering around the entrance hall doors.

'You're quite sure they weren't taken to the wrong classroom?' Kale was asking, drumming his fingers impatiently on the counter top. 'I've scoured the entire science block and there's not a sign. I told Mrs Willow to expect them and have them delivered to Mr Penter's lab in readiness. I simply fail to see how a box of rats which arrived by special delivery can completely disappear!'

'I keep telling you, I'm just a temp!' complained the receptionist; perhaps extra tetchy now her phone call had been interrupted. 'All I know is that something from Cryo Laboratories was delivered this morning at 8.17 a.m. and the real receptionist signed for it. But with her away at some special clinic and not here to ask, I honestly can't tell you what happened to it!'

'When is Mrs Willow back?' huffed Kale.

'She's supposed to be back at lunchtime. But what do I know?' The receptionist leaned forward and glared at him defiantly. 'I'm only a temp!'

'Thanks for your time,' muttered Kale, before stomping off.

By the time Sam had reached the reception counter, the temp was back having a moan on the phone. He dropped off the keys, then hurried away.

His only problem now was staying out of sight of any other wandering teachers until the bell went for lunchtime. He tried to walk with an air of knowing just where he was going and just what he was doing. One teacher surprised him by bursting out of a nearby doorway, but he gave her a cheery smile and she didn't bother him.

It was while Sam was congratulating himself on his performance that he glimpsed Penter at the end of the corridor. If he kept coming, they would be on a collision course!

Sam turned on his heel and walked speedily back the way he had come. But a split-second later, his heart sank. At the entrance hall end of the passage, Cabbage Kale had appeared. His head was thrown back in an extravagant yawn, the dimple in his chin trained on Sam like a little black eye.

Sam cut into the same doorway the other teacher had sprung from. Luckily the room was empty—from the stack of books on the desk, she must have been doing some marking. Maybe she'd slipped out to the loo—in which case, she might come back any time . . .

Sure enough, outside, he could hear three sets of footsteps, all of them coming closer. If he was caught now . . .

The window was open wide beside the desk, and Sam quickly clambered through it. But the belt loop of his trousers snagged on the catch. He was stuck.

 93

To his horror, the classroom door began to open.

With strength born of desperation Sam pulled himself free and fell out through the window—right into a prickly hedge. He held himself dead still. If the teacher had heard him and looked out of the window to investigate . . .

But no face appeared.

Slowly, painstakingly, Sam disentangled himself and crawled away, keeping close to the wall so no one could see him through the foliage or the window. It was baking hot, and he was soon sweating like a pig in an oven. The prickly leaves and branches snagged on his clothes and scratched his skin. His mum had often accused him of looking as if he'd been dragged through a hedge backwards. If she could only see him now . . .

His legs were beginning to ache from walking all crouched up so he stopped for a second. A voice he recognized floated out from somewhere close by. It was Ruthless Cook, and she was reading something—very slowly:

'By the pricking of my thumbs, something wicked this way comes.'

Raising an eyebrow, Sam came to a halt. 'By the

scratching of my toe, how exactly did *she* know?' he quipped; he was *totally* wicked, after all.

'How now, you secret, black and midnight hags . . .' came a male voice, bold and confident—it sounded like Fido Tennant. Clearly Sam had approached his own English class from the outside. Peering through the window, he saw Sara and Memphis sitting at the back corner of the class. The window beside them was open— if only there hadn't been a thick, spreading bush planted just outside he could have crept close enough to whisper them a progress report.

Then again, in this modern technological age, there were other ways of communicating. Sam pulled out a sheet of paper from his bag, wrote his message and then stared thoughtfully at the white rectangle. He only hoped Ruth's brief demonstration of paper aeronautics had made more impact on him than the lessons from Penter and Kale . . .

Sara was terminally bored, sharing Memphis's copy of *Macbeth* and trying to follow the tongue-twisting language.

 95

She'd just lasted through a long, gruesome list of magic spell ingredients, including the finger of a 'birth-strangled babe', which wasn't really what she wanted to think about after recent events. And now Macbeth was confronting a load of old witches on a heath somewhere. Sara was reminded of the time her dad had come back drunk from a football match to find Mum having a barbecue with her mates in the garden.

Ruth made a pretty good witch—in looks and attitude if not in speech—and Fido was impressive as Macbeth, definitely leading man material. She was daydreaming about playing Juliet opposite his Romeo in some huge-budget film remake when something blew through the window and landed right in front of her on the desk.

She blinked. It was a paper plane—one that had been folded and unfolded in different places about ten times by the look of it, but to a pretty impressive plan. There was no one outside the window, but since Ruth was in witch-mode it could only have come from Sam.

'He knows thy thought,' read the girl playing First Witch. 'Hear his speech but say thou nought.'

Good thinking, thought Sara. Straight away, Memphis covered the paper with one large hand. As the class turned over the page of *Macbeth*, she used the cover of rustling to unfold the plane.

There was a message:

No fingers in sick room—no ice packs either. Maybe suspect took ice packs to stop fingers going off? I'm going off my head—hate unsolved mysteries! Lunchtime—got to find Colin Cox.
—S

Sara gave Memphis a look, then took the KICK MY BUTT sign and turned it over. She wrote on the back:

See this paper stuck to Thumb-chum's back—maybe by Colin Cox. Special delivery?
—S

Then she started folding it into a crappier but hopefully still airworthy plane.

97

'All right, we'll pause there a moment,' said Miss Bedfellow as Fido's Macbeth finished moaning about having three ears or something. 'What's so wonderful about this play is its incredible, blood-soaked use of imagery.'

Sara's stomach squirmed. She'd *so* had enough of blood.

'For instance,' Mrs Bedfellow went on. '"By the pricking of my thumbs . . ." Who can tell me what that means?'

'Ask Ashley,' joked someone, 'he's the thumb expert!'

The class laughed, and Miss Bedfellow spared Ashley a withering look. 'Get your thumb out of your mouth,' she told him, and reluctantly he obeyed. 'You know, in Shakespeare's time, the thumb was used in good luck blessings. If you were passing the house of a witch, for instance, you held your thumb against your palm. And when someone died, their thumbs were turned down to stop evil spirits taking hold of their bodies.'

'Ugh, who'd want to hold the thumb-chum's body?' Ruth Cook snorted, to an outburst of giggles.

Straight away, Ashley's thumb flew straight back to his mouth.

'Shut up, Ruth, or you'll be standing outside,' snapped Miss Bedfellow. 'So—to prick a thumb and make it bleed could be seen as a way to spoil a blessing . . .' She trailed off as she noticed Ashley again. 'What did I just tell you? Thumb *out*!'

Ashley sighed and thrust his hands into his pockets. A moment later, he pulled out his right hand and looked at it.

Then he gave an almighty yell and threw both hands in the air.

Everyone stared at Ashley, astounded. Except for Sara and Memphis.

Something had plopped down on their desk from nowhere.

It was a severed thumb—grey, wet, and cleanly cut.

Ashley ran screaming from the room, while Sara's first thought was to throw up. While she grabbed her stomach, Memphis grabbed the thumb and laid it in the lengthways fold of Sara's paper plane, before tossing the whole lot out of the window.

Two seconds later, Sara threw most of her breakfast after it.

Sam watched in horror as Sara performed her technicoloured yawn. Now he was very grateful the bush had blocked a closer approach. He'd jumped at Ashley's scream, then blinked as a very rubbishy plane nosedived out of the window. But what had set Sara honking—what was going on? He tried to signal to her, but she quickly wiped her mouth and ducked back inside.

As Sam searched for the plane, he listened in on the classroom confusion, hoping to learn more.

'Calm down, you lot,' shouted Miss Bedfellow over the hubbub. 'Sara, what are you doing?'

'Nothing, miss,' said Sara, clearing her throat. 'Just . . . uh . . . thought that something outside might have scared him. But there's nothing worth seeing out there.'

Charming, thought Sam.

'What made him react like that?' enquired Miss Bedfellow. She sounded completely suspicious. 'Are you sure you didn't see anything?'

100

'Nothing, miss.'

'Did you, Memphis?'

'Maybe he saw a spider or something,' suggested Memphis. 'He *is* a bit of a baby. Hey, maybe that's it! Maybe he's teething!'

'Thounded pretty therious to me,' said Fido, and the class was in uproar once again.

'The next person to make a sound gets detention every lunchtime until they die!' yelled Miss Bedfellow.

Suddenly, you could hear a pin drop. Sam only hoped you couldn't hear a guy unfolding a paper plane. He'd found it in the undergrowth at last (no proper guidance, these amateur jobs), and inside it was . . .

Ugh. His breakfast almost went the same way as Sara's at the sight of the plane's grey stumpy pilot. Or maybe it had just thumbed a lift . . .

Sam let the thumb fall to the ground and stared at it sadly. 'You start off just chewing your nails, then see what happens.' Quickly, he read Sara's message and studied the delivery note. Very interesting . . . how many more digits, index fingers, thumbs or otherwise might be lurking somewhere in the school?

Suddenly he heard running feet. Wrapping the thumb in the paper plane, he shoved it in his pocket and peered through the undergrowth to see who was coming.

It was Ashley, white-faced and running full-pelt, as if an axe-murderer was right behind him.

'Hey, Ashley!' he hissed, waving a hand out of the bushes. 'It's me, Sam!'

Ashley skidded to a halt and looked at him suspiciously.

'You're making enough noise to get every teacher in the school on our backs,' he whispered. 'Come on, we'll find a place to hide out together.'

'Why would you want to help me?' squeaked Ashley.

'Uh . . .' Sam groped around for a good reason not involving chopped-off fingers. 'Uh . . . 'Cause we're detention buddies! Two of a kind! Come on, I'll make sure we're not caught. I hope.'

Sam sneaked out of the bushes and ran ahead down the wide path, Ashley wheezing along behind him. Soon they reached a separate block with an outside stairwell. One whiff of burgers and cake told him this was the canteen block.

He could hear cooks and servers clattering around inside the big kitchens, getting ready for the lunchtime rush.

Then suddenly he ducked out of sight behind a bench and pulled Ashley down with him, as a red-faced, formidable looking woman stomped from around the corner of the block.

'Did you catch him?' called one of the servers inside the canteen kitchens.

'No, got away, the little tyke,' said the woman, marching inside the kitchens. 'One of the year tens, I think. Speedy little sods, they are.'

Sam frowned. Clearly he and Ashley weren't the only fugitives at Freekham right now.

'Cheek of 'em, sneaking in here to poke about,' came a moaning male voice.

'Probably just hungry,' someone suggested.

'If that's true, this is the *last* place he'd come,' muttered Sam. He ran across to the stairwell with Ashley and led him halfway up. Then he crouched and dragged Ashley down beside him so that the wall of the stairway shielded them from view.

'Why weren't you in class, anyway?' panted Ashley.

'I fell out with a teacher. Out through the window, in fact,' Sam explained. 'What happened in there? Why the commotion?'

'I found . . .' Ashley started shaking. He went to put his thumb back in his mouth but Sam batted it away. 'I found a chopped-off thumb in my pocket! A real one!'

Sam gasped as if this was a revelation. If Ashley knew what *he* knew, the lad might think Sam was responsible and clam up. 'You sure it was real?'

'For definite.'

'Why didn't you show Miss Bedfellow?'

'I was too busy running away.'

'A thumb, huh?' said Sam. 'So *that's* what I saw falling out of the window.'

'Out of the window?' echoed Ashley, his face crumpled and crestfallen. 'Then I've got no proof. People will never stop laughing at me!'

'I have the same problem. It's tough when you're a natural born comedian.' Sam grew more serious. 'Ashley, how did a severed thumb get in your pocket?'

'Someone must have put it there,' whimpered Ashley. 'Whoever stuck the note on my back, I bet.'

'Did you see them?'

'No. But someone must really hate me!'

Sam shrugged. 'Maybe they thought you might like a bit of variety—a third thumb to suck.'

Ashley scowled. 'Why does everyone pick on me?'

'Probably since you offer them so much scope.'

'It's true,' Ashley agreed sadly. 'Even if I *did* give up my thumb, I'd still suck big time around here. It's too late to change.'

'It's never too late to change,' Sam told him, before smiling wryly. 'Then again, I've changed house, school, and county roughly three times each year. It's never too *early* to change as far as I'm concerned, so what do I know?' He looked at Ashley seriously. 'One thing I *do* know. Whoever did this has gone to a lot of trouble. Did you stop to think this could be a warning?'

'A warning?' whimpered Ashley.

'Sure. If you don't stop sucking your thumbs, you'll get them chopped off!'

Ashley's big baby face went snowy white and his lower lip started to wobble. He looked as if he might burst into tears or wet himself—or probably both.

105

'Come on, Ashley,' said Sam firmly. 'Pull your-self together. I'm sure it won't come to that. Now, tell me more about that box you were carrying this morning.'

'What's to tell?' moped Ashley. 'Like I said, it was full of old textbooks for the charity cupboard in Hayes's room.'

'*Only* textbooks? Did you look *inside* the box?'

'Course not. Why would I have done?'

'So it's possible that the guy who was helping you—Colin Cox, right?—could have slipped something inside the box . . .'

'Who cares about that dumb old box of books!' hissed Ashley.

'Have you seen Colin since then?'

'Yeah. He had a go at me at breather. Then my brother showed up. For one second I thought maybe he was sticking up for me.' He sighed. 'But it was just a trick. My brother *never* sticks up for me in public. If he did, he reckons people would start picking on him too. At the end of the day, I guess he likes Colin more than me. I guess he's ashamed of his little brother.'

'So it was most likely Colin who planted that KICK MY BUTT sign on your back,' Sam mused,

106

thinking of Sara's note. 'And he might just have planted something else while he was about it.' Sam rubbed his hands together. 'Ashley, things seem to be falling into place—as well as into your pocket!'

Lunchtime

It was a relief to Sam when the lunchtime siren went off. Suddenly the paths and open spaces around Freekham's many minor buildings were filled with people, and he and Ashley weren't sticking out like . . .

Well. Like sore thumbs.

'You must have computers here, right?' asked Sam, walking back down the concrete steps to join the thronging crowds.

'Lots.' Ashley nodded and pointed to a nearby building. 'The computer lab's in that block.'

'Can we get online there?'

'Yes, if you have a password.'

'Do you have a password?'

'No.'

'Well, I'll just have to see if I can get one.' Sam sighed. 'Just hang around here and try to stay out of sight. And stop sucking that thumb!'

Sam abandoned him with some relief. Ashley would be teacher-target number one after his little performance in English, while Sam was still pretty much an unknown—hopefully he could get away with a lot more . . .

His confidence was boosted as his luck held— he met no teachers or classmates on his way to the block that housed the computer lab.

Until he got there.

Though there were seats and computers for ten users, only two people were sitting in the white-panelled room: a kid with blue-framed glasses and his number one fan—the one-and-only Minger Harris. Hunched over the computer like a squirrel over a nut, she didn't look up as Sam walked in.

'Hey,' said Sam.

The girl almost jumped out of her seat, staring around in alarm. Then she saw it was Sam and she blushed and smiled nervously. She opened her mouth but nothing came out.

'Are you logged on?' he asked.

She nodded.

'You've got a password, great. Enjoying a little surf, huh?'

She shrugged.

'Looking at anything cool?' he asked gamely. But it was just the Google front page, with no query typed in; she wasn't browsing anywhere. Sam felt a sudden wave of sympathy. He cleared his throat. 'I guess it's just quieter in here than out there, right?'

She nodded.

'Look, do you have a first name?' he wondered. 'I don't really want to call you "Minger".'

The girl blinked at him. She had amber eyes and was quite cute in a dweeby kind of way. 'Michelle,' she whispered.

'Michelle, would you mind if I sneaked on your computer and looked something up quickly?' he asked.

Looking slightly dazed, Michelle nodded and scrambled out of her seat. Sam grinned at her and plonked himself down, his fingers skittering over the keyboard.

CRYO LABORATORIES, he typed as his query, then hit return.

A few seconds later he was clicking the link to their homepage. Seemed Cryo Labs was more than just a supplier of biological bits and pieces for schools and industries—they were involved in cutting edge scientific research, and sponsored special clinics around the country where pioneering experimental surgery was tested on volunteers. And one of those clinics was fairly local.

Sam's eyes narrowed. That frizzy-haired temp had said something to Cabbage Kale about the real receptionist: *'with her away at some special clinic and not here to ask . . .'*

A box full of fingers and a receptionist with one hand. Could the two be linked?

He went back a page to Google and typed in: HAND TRANSPLANTS.

The search results duly appeared. There hadn't been many hand transplants—only a couple performed in America, with partial success. He clicked on another link. One guy had the fingers from his left hand stitched on to the right for reasons too gory to look into closely.

But it opened a whole lot of possibilities.

'Pioneering experimental surgery . . .' breathed Sam, 'but a really rubbish postal service.' He stood up and smiled at Michelle Harris. 'Thanks for sharing.'

She shrugged and smiled back. But that 'my hero' look was creeping back into her amber eyes, and the last thing Sam wanted on his first day was a reputation as geek love-god. It was time to beat a hasty retreat and find Sara and Memphis.

But Sam paused in the exit before stepping out into the sweltering sunshine—trouble was coming his way. It was Ruthless Cook, passing by the block with a couple of cronies. She saw Sam in the doorway. Bringing one of her mates with her, she started heading straight for him.

'Uh-oh,' he muttered, fresh sweat breaking out on his forehead.

'Oi! Innocent!' she called. A worrying leer he took to be a smile was thick on her face. 'You bunked off last lesson, didn't you?'

'You mean that *wasn't* lunch break?' Sam stared at her in pretend horror. 'I thought it was kind of quiet.'

'You've got some guts,' she said admiringly, 'bunking off on your first day when you've already had a detention.'

'Yeah, nice one,' added her mate, a big, dumpy girl nursing a set of bruised knuckles.

'You missed out though—Thumb-chum threw

a fit,' added Ruth. 'He went running out the room like a cat with a firework up its—'

'Did he? What a loser.'

'I reckon he's just mental.' Ruth took a step closer. 'It's *you* I don't get, Innocent. One minute you act like a complete prat, the next like . . .'

'A prat with something missing?'

'No. Like . . . Well, like you're all right.' Ruth and Knuckles advanced on him, and Sam found himself backing away inside the block, towards the computer room. 'I thought we might be able to have a laugh together. Were you really into in my planes? Or just trying it on?'

'I promise I would never knowingly try it on with you, Ruth,' said Sam with feeling.

She and her Neanderthal mate sniggered. 'So is this where you hid to get out of English?' Ruth asked.

'Uh, no. I just got here.'

'You want to watch out. The computer lab's just there—Geek Central. Only total nerds hang out . . .'

She trailed off as she looked into the computer room and saw Michelle Harris cowering inside with crimson cheeks.

113

'Well, well,' said Ruth, folding her arms. 'What have we here?'

'Oh, hey, Michelle!' Sam gave a weak wave. 'Didn't see you!'

'Don't give me that, Innocent,' snarled Ruth, very firmly back in Ruthless mode. 'You stuck up for Minger Harris before.'

'He fancies her,' deduced Knuckles.

'Yeah, you fancy her,' Ruth agreed. 'And you hung out with Thumb-chum at break. I bet he ran out of class to go looking for you.'

Sam felt like a petty crook being fitted up for the crime of the century. 'It's an interesting theory, but—'

'You, him, and Minger have, like, really sad parties together,' Knuckles suggested.

Ruth laughed. 'Yeah, you minger-loving geek-brain.'

'Oh, get out of my face, Ruth,' said Sam, losing patience. 'You may not have anything better to do than sling names at people, but *I* do.'

He tried to push past her but Knuckles blocked his way. Then suddenly Ruth grabbed hold of him and slammed him up against the wall. He gasped, more with shock than with pain.

 114

'No one tries to make me look stupid,' said Ruth quietly.

'No one needs to try,' Sam retorted. 'You do a great job all by yourself.'

She drew back her fist. Sam tried to break free of her grip, but found he couldn't. What he'd taken for lard on Ruthless was actually muscle. He'd underestimated her, and his face was about to pay the price . . .

Then he jumped at the sound of a ferocious, startling shriek. Ruth froze, mid-swing.

'Leave him alone!'

It was Michelle Harris.

Sam stared in amazement. Michelle had bunched her fists and looked mega-furious. Only her trembling bottom lip gave away the fact she was terrified.

Ruth snapped out of her surprise and snorted with laughter. 'Stay out of this, Minger. You can kiss your boyfriend better when I've rearranged his face.'

But further help was to come from an unexpected source. 'Teacher!' hissed Knuckles. 'Coming this way. He must have heard the minger shouting.'

Ruth reluctantly released Sam and jabbed a finger at Michelle. 'Since you're so bothered, *you* can get a beating in your boyfriend's place,' she hissed. 'Top of the school drive after last period. Be there. And if I have to come looking, I'll make it twenty times worse for you.'

The teacher came in, a shabbily dressed man with a head like a hard-boiled egg and a moustache you could clean your shoes with.

'What's going on here?' he asked suspiciously. Sam didn't blame him—there were five people in the computer lab and only the kid with glasses was actually looking at a screen while the rest were loitering with red faces.

'Michelle saw a spider, sir, and she screamed,' said Sam quickly. 'I was about to squash it, but she thought I should . . . Well, you heard her: *leave him alone.*'

'I see,' said the teacher, in the kind of voice that suggested he didn't see anything at all. 'Well, come on, you should all know the rules. Anyone who's not signed into the computer lab with a password should leave right now.'

'Good idea,' said Sam. He held the door open and gestured to Ruth and her mate. 'Come on, guys, let's get going. Oh, and thanks, Michelle. I owe you one.'

Michelle looked at him and shrugged helplessly.

'I owe her too,' said Ruth with a tight smile. 'But don't worry. I'll make sure she gets it later.'

With the teacher watching them beadily from the doorway, Ruth and Knuckles went in one direction while Sam sped off in another.

Great, he thought. He'd found out where the fingers may have come from, but he'd managed to get Michelle Harris into trouble at the same time. He'd have to think of some way to get her off the hook . . .

'Sam!' hissed a nervous voice from a nearby bush. 'It's Ashley!'

Sam frowned. 'Hey, *I'm* the one who hides in bushes. You could show *some* imagination!'

'I just realized,' he said. 'When I ran out I left my bag in Bedfellow's room! It's got our detentions in—we're meant to hand them in to Penter, remember? If we don't, he'll probably take us to the Head!'

'That,' said Sam, 'is the least of my problems.'

* * *

117

Sara wasn't sure how Memphis had persuaded her to come to the canteen for lunch. Her stomach was feeling more delicate than a house of cards in an earthquake, and the rich smell of burgers and fried onions was threatening to flatten it for good.

'You should definitely eat, you'll feel better for it,' said Memphis. 'And we're first sitting, so we have the pick of the menu.'

'Lucky us,' said Sara.

'Shall I get you some soup or something?'

'The something sounds more appetizing.' Sara sighed and handed Memphis some coins from her purse. 'Go on, then. Surprise me.'

'I'll leave that to *him*,' Memphis said, glancing at the door behind her before setting off to join the queue. Sara turned to see Sam Innocent sneaking into the canteen through the back way, Ashley just behind him, thumb in mouth.

Sara didn't say anything, just looked at them both expectantly.

'Well,' said Sam. 'I've sure been having some fun.'

'Did you see what happened to my bag?' blurted Ashley abruptly. 'I left it in Bedfellow's room.'

118

'Then it'll still be there,' said Sara. 'Sorry, Ashley, guess no one thought to pick it up. Not even Bedfellow.'

'She'll be looking for me,' fretted Ashley. 'I can't just go and pick it up, can I? She could be waiting for me! And if I don't, then Penter will kill me for not doing my lines! And Sam too!'

'He'll probably kill me anyway for not taking detention seriously,' mused Sam. 'Look, tell you what, Ashley, I'll pick it up for you after lunch. That way you can avoid awkward questions till you're feeling stronger. Go get some lunch in the meantime.'

Ashley popped his thumb back in his mouth. 'Can I sit with you guys?'

Sam clicked his tongue and looked apologetic. 'Sorry, mate. I think Memphis was saving these two seats for a friend of hers . . .' He pointed to the next table but one. 'How about you sit just over there?'

'OK,' said Ashley sadly, and trudged off to take his place at the back of the queue.

'Phew!' breathed Sam. 'That got rid of him!'

'Wasn't very nice, was it?' muttered Sara.

'But safer for all concerned,' Sam countered.

'Especially if I run into Ruthless Cook again. Don't want any more geeks taking the flak for me . . .' She frowned at him, puzzled, but he held up a hand as if he didn't want to talk about it. 'Anyway, I didn't see you arguing. Tell you what, if you feel so bad, *you* go get his bag for him.'

'I will, too,' said Sara stoutly. Her stomach felt extra-gripey, and she rubbed it gently.

Sam eyed her for a moment or two. 'You must be feeling pretty bad, huh?'

Sara gave him a small smile. 'A little less puke-some now, thanks.'

'No, I meant you must feeling bad after making such a pathetic paper plane in Bedfellow's class!' he teased.

She smiled despite herself. 'I'm hoping that after maybe two or three years of counselling I'll get over it. So what have you found out?'

'Wait for me,' said Memphis, returning with a plate of salad for Sara.

They both listened closely as Sam recounted his conversation with Ashley and what he'd discovered in the computer lab. Memphis nodded to herself as if she had secretly known all along.

 120

'So, *I* reckon that someone in Cryo Labs' supply depot mixed up their packages,' Sam concluded. 'The clinic got Kale's rats, and Freekham High got the clinic's fingers.'

'So you think Cryo Labs are, like, doing experiments on fingers and stuff?' said Sara. 'On people like Mrs Willow, the receptionist?'

'Would make sense of her being away at this special clinic,' said Sam. 'She's a volunteer.'

'A guinea pig, more like,' added Sara. She nibbled some cucumber but her stomach protested, and she pushed the plate aside. Sam wasted no time helping himself.

'It would make sense of something else,' said Memphis. 'I've seen Colin Cox get lifts to school with Mrs Willow some days. If he came in with her this morning, he'd have got to school early.'

Sam nodded. 'Kale's package was signed for at 8.17 according to the temp,' he said through a mouthful of lettuce and tomato, 'by Mrs Willow. And get this. Cabbage Kale had asked her the day before to have the parcel delivered to Penter's room, ready for his lesson this morning.'

'And who's the obvious choice to play delivery

121

boy?' Memphis realized. 'Good ol' Colin! But why would he open up the parcel?'

'Who knows?' said Sam. 'But we know what he found inside.'

'One ended up in the bin, one he used to scare Ashley.' Sara frowned. 'But how many more defrosting digits were there in that parcel?'

'And where are they now?' Sam wondered.

As he spoke, Ashley trudged past, dejected. Sara watched him sit down to eat his lunch: a burnt baked potato half-afloat in a crusty sea of baked beans. Two girls who were sitting at his table whispered fiercely, then got up and left him sitting alone. Ashley made out he hadn't noticed.

But someone else soon came visiting—a familiar red-faced, brown-haired figure with shifty eyes. He parked his bum on the table beside Ashley and started talking quietly.

'Sam, that's the faker I ran into in the sickroom,' said Sara. 'Turns out he's Ashley's brother.'

'Who never sticks up for him,' Sam recalled.

'He did today,' said Memphis, 'sort of. When Colin was giving Ashley hassle before English, Roger stepped in.'

 122

'Yeah, and showed some real brotherly shove,' Sara added. 'Didn't take the sign off Ashley's back, though, did he?'

'He's got his own reputation to think about,' Memphis pointed out. 'Can't be easy, being big brother to the school dweeb.'

'You're *such* a loser,' snarled Roger suddenly, stomping away from Ashley's table towards the exit. 'And keep that dumb thumb out of your mouth!'

Sam raised his eyebrows. 'Apparently not!'

'Poor old Ashley,' sighed Sara, watching him turn back to his baked potato, all alone once more. 'Look, guys, school joke or not, this thing is getting serious. Putting a chopped off thumb in Ashley's pocket goes way beyond a bit of bullying! Should we split on Colin Cox?'

'What, tell Penter or something?' Sam looked uneasy. 'I don't know. Not until we have some real evidence that he's involved, anyway.' A thought seemed to occur to him. 'Oh yeah, speaking of evidence, I've still got that thumb. It's in *my* pocket, now.'

'That thing is in your *pocket*?' hissed Sara, appalled.

He shrugged. 'It's all right, I rolled the delivery note around it first.'

'Oh, well, that's all right then,' said Memphis drily. 'So long as it's wrapped up, that's not at all—'

'GROSS!' came a shrill cry from across the canteen.

'I hate it when people finish my sentences,' remarked Memphis.

'What's going on?' said Sara worriedly. A bunch of girls had jumped up from their chairs as if they were fitted with ejector seats, and one of them was pointing at her plate. A sudden, nervous hush settled over the canteen.

'There's something in my custard!' shouted one of the girls. 'It's like a big slug!'

An excited buzz swept through the canteen.

Memphis looked amused. 'Knowing the kind of stuff they serve up here, it probably *is* a big slug.'

But Sara had a sinking feeling. 'Unless . . .'

'Someone get rid of it!' yelled the girl. 'It's a slug, it's a slug!'

'Let's have a look.' That was Fido, gallantly striding to the rescue.

124

'Don't be ridiculous,' said a skinny dinner lady striding across to see. 'Everyone stay calm, it's probably just . . . just a . . .' She stared, transfixed, at the plate.

The noise in the canteen drained away as swiftly as the colour from her face. An expectant hush settled over the canteen as Fido picked up a spoon and pushed it into the custard.

Then Sara jumped at a fresh shout just across from her. It was Ashley, flapping in panic.

'Help!' he bawled. 'Thumbs! *There are human thumbs in my baked potato!*'

Sara felt the hairs standing up on the back of her neck.

'And this isn't a slug,' cried Fido, holding up the spoon. 'It's a finger!'

The dinner lady covered her mouth with both hands. But she couldn't hold in a slimy spray of sick that spattered over the girls' table. At the same time, the girl who had made the discovery hurled all over the floor. Desperate to avoid splashing, Fido jumped backwards, and the custardy finger flew from his spoon to land in another boy's gravy. This boy recoiled and threw up all over himself.

 125

But then Sara's eyes were tugged away from this gruesome vomit ballet by a horrible, blocked-drainpipe sound coming from Ashley as he blew chunks all over the table next to him. The unlucky diners shrieked and yelled.

And suddenly the canteen was ringing with retching and awash with vomit. Chairs scraped, people slipped and slid on the floor and panicking cries rose in number and volume.

'I've found a finger in my hot dog!'

'That's a sausage, stupid.'

'But *that's* a thumb!'

'Show me! Where? Where?'

'Omigod, omigod, omigod, omigod . . .'

'I found one too!'

'Don't puke on me! Hold it in! Hold it—uuugggghhhhh . . .'

'Sara! Look out!' yelled Memphis.

Stunned, Sara saw a huge, towering guy staggering white-faced like a zombie towards her. He'd speared a finger on his fork and looked set to lose his guts. She stared with a horrified fascination as his cheeks started to bulge . . .

But at the last moment, someone dragged her

 126

clear. It was Sam. 'Out of here!' he cried. 'Memphis, come on!'

Sara kept her head down and her hands over her ears and Sam led her from the chaos in the canteen.

As he staggered out of the door, Sara and Memphis close behind, Sam prayed and prayed that he wouldn't be sick too.

'Thanks, Sam,' said Sara shakily. 'My head may not have forgiven you for that bump, but my stomach lets you off completely.'

'If only I'd brought my camcorder with me,' gasped Fido, running out behind them. 'That was a movie in itself! I'd win prizes for the special effects!' He paused for a moment, looking at Sam and Sara. 'Weird how nothing like this ever happened before—until *you* two arrive.'

'We had nothing to do with it!' Sara protested.

'But we're going to find out who did,' added Sam.

'When you do, ask them if they can stage it again next week,' grinned Fido. 'I'll have my camcorder ready.' Then off he went, cool and solitary.

Unpleasant noises were still carrying from beyond the canteen doors, so Sam and the girls swiftly decided to move on too. They kept going till they got to the edge of the main playground, leaving the clamour and upchuck of the canteen far behind them.

'That was the grossest thing I ever saw in my life,' said Memphis who, like Fido, actually seemed impressed in a weird kind of way. 'When the Head finds out about this, he's going to blow megatons.'

Sara nodded, her eyes wide. 'How did Colin Cox organize *that*?'

'I think I know,' said Sam slowly. 'Ashley and me were hiding out around here earlier. One of the supervisors was complaining about some kid poking around the kitchens . . . Colin must have sneaked the digits into the food trays somehow.'

'But how did he make sure Ashley got thumbs in his jacket potato?' wondered Sara.

'Luck of the draw?' guessed Memphis.

'Blanket bombing,' was Sam's theory. 'You saw what it was like in there—fingers and thumbs everywhere. I'm only surprised your salad didn't come with a side order of pickled pinkie.'

128

'Leave it,' Sara commanded. 'I barely held on to my guts back there, don't make me sick now.'

'We have to find Colin Cox,' said Sam. 'He's got some questions to answer.'

'And Roger too,' Memphis announced.

Sam frowned. 'Why him?'

She shrugged and nodded over his shoulder. 'I'd ask him, why are two guys who've been best mates for years suddenly fighting like worst enemies?'

Sam turned to see a savage scrum had formed outside the school tennis courts. Surrounded by a cheering, jeering crowd, Roger Lamb and the mysterious Colin Cox were having a real scrap, fists flying, knees dangerously close to groins and everything.

'Come on,' said Sam, sprinting off.

'What's the sudden rush?' called Sara.

He stopped running, turned and stared at her like she was crazy. 'It's a *fight*! You want to miss it?'

'Duh!' Sara cried in response. 'You want to *watch* it?'

'In pursuit of the truth—you try and stop me!' said Sam. 'Besides, with Ruthless about, I need

129

to pick up tips.' And off he ran, leaving the two girls behind.

'Oi! Oi! Oi!' the crowd was chanting, clapping their hands and whistling as the two guys grappled. By the time Sam got there, Colin looked as if he'd had enough and was struggling to get away. But Roger had gripped hold of his mate's blazer, and looked to be trying to rip it off his back.

Sam frowned. What was Colin Cox doing wearing a blazer in this heat anyway?

'Get off me!' roared Colin.

'Mine!' bellowed Roger. 'Give me!'

With a loud ripping noise, Colin's blazer was torn away. Roger yelled in triumph as Colin overbalanced and fell sprawling to the concrete. A big cheer went up from the gathered crowd.

'Teacher!' someone hissed in warning.

In a moment Roger was running like a dog after a rabbit, and the crowd started to break up. Sam turned to see two red-faced teachers striding across the playground, ignoring Roger the moving target and zeroing in on the scene of the crime. You'd think they'd have their hands full trying to cope with calming down the grisly scene in the canteen . . .

130

But one thing was for sure—every teacher in Freekham would now be in a mood fouler than those contaminated baked beans. Sam decided this was not a good time to be caught—especially when he had a soggy severed thumb of his own in his pocket!

He quickly stooped to help up Colin, who was still sprawled on the ground. 'You OK, Colin? Let me give you a hand there.'

'How'd you know my name?' Colin asked gruffly. 'I don't know you, do I?'

'Nope, but I expect you know those two teachers coming our way,' said Sam. 'How'd you feel about making a sharp exit?'

'Eat my dust,' Colin muttered.

He sprinted away, Sam hot on his heels, as the teachers gave chase.

'Stop following me, kid,' Colin hissed, throwing a warning look over his shoulder.

'I was hoping to have a quick chat,' panted Sam. His shirt was clinging to his back already with sweat. 'What's with that blazer thing on a day like this? You feel the cold, Colin?'

'Maybe I do,' he grunted. 'Push off.'

They turned a corner and ran out on the top

of the school drive. Sam pictured poor Michelle Harris standing here after school, quaking like a jelly at the sight of Ruthless Cook coming to get her. There had to be something he could do . . .

Later. He couldn't be distracted from interrogating his prime suspect, who even now was making for the cycle sheds.

Sam put on an extra spurt of speed and reached the sheds' safety slightly ahead of Colin. There was no sign of any teachers in pursuit, and the two of them collapsed against a wall, panting like greyhounds after a race.

'Tell, me, Colin,' Sam gasped, 'was it you who found the fingers?'

Colin looked suddenly very afraid. 'Don't know what you're talking about.'

'I think you do,' said Sam. 'And I think Mrs Willow the receptionist will know too.'

Colin got up and glowered at Sam. 'Keep your nose out of my business.'

'Keep your fingers and thumbs out of everyone else's!' Sam retorted. 'I got a detention thanks to you. But I'm on to you now, see? First Ashley, then the canteen—what's your next trick going to be?'

'You don't know nothing,' stormed Colin.

Sam was about to point out that this was a double negative and implied he knew everything—which was far closer to the truth. But Colin had run off again.

Sara watched Roger Lamb run past with the blazer, his tattered trophy. He was red-faced and had scratches on his cheek—but there was no mistaking the triumphant look in his eyes.

'Funny,' said Memphis. 'What does he want with a blazer, anyway?'

'Who knows or cares,' sighed Sara. 'This is officially the weirdest day of my whole life.'

'And it's only lunchtime,' said Memphis darkly.

'Come on, let's go get Ashley's bag back from Miss Bedfellow's classroom,' said Sara. 'I told Sam I would, Ashley needs it back.'

'Then I guess we'll have to find Ashley, too,' said Memphis. 'Last seen proving to the school he's got guts after all, by splashing them all over the table.'

As they walked past the canteen a hideous sicky smell filled the air. Sara saw a mass of

133

stunned, silent, or sobbing pupils wandering about outside. Some of them were mopping at their spattered uniforms with wet cloths. There was no sign of Ashley; perhaps he'd got away. A whole truckload of stern-faced teachers milled about like riot police, firing off questions and taking notes on little pads.

'Heads will roll for this one,' Memphis reckoned.

'Aren't there enough severed body parts around right now?' said Sara, quickening her pace before they were roped in for questioning too.

When they reached Miss Bedfellow's room, they found just one person inside—Roger. He was out of breath, still clutching the blazer, and crouching over Ashley's rucksack.

Memphis folded her arms. 'What are you doing here?'

'Getting my brother's bag for him,' he growled. 'What's it to you?'

'Where is he, then?' asked Sara. 'Last time we saw him he was throwing up all over the place with a baked potato full of thumbs.'

'He's hiding in the bogs now,' said Roger, 'feeling well sorry for himself.'

 134

'Can't say I blame him,' said Sara. 'By the way, your ankle's got a lot better since this morning, hasn't it? Playing footie, fighting, running . . .'

'Yeah, well,' said Roger. 'Fast healer, aren't I?'

'Why take Colin Cox's blazer?' asked Memphis. 'You feel the cold or something?'

'I thought you were fainting with the heat earlier,' Sara added.

'Mind your own business.' Roger headed for the door but Sara stepped sideways to block his way.

'I told Ashley *I'd* get his bag,' said Sara. 'Why did he ask you?'

''Cause I told him you were just messing with his head,' said Roger. 'You're trying to play some pathetic trick on him, right?'

'Wrong.'

'Come off it,' Roger sneered. 'A girl like you really wants to help my little brother? You think he's a joke, just like all the rest.'

'You were hardly acting the caring brother back in the canteen,' Memphis pointed out. 'You called him a loser!'

'He *is* a loser,' said Roger. 'But he doesn't need people like *you* making him look a bigger one.'

 135

Sara folded her arms. 'What about your mate Colin? He doesn't—'

'Colin Cox is not my mate, all right?' Roger barged past them. 'Ashley needs to grow up and sort himself out. And so do stupid little girls like you.'

He stalked out through the door.

'Well, that's us "stupid little girls" told,' said Memphis sourly.

Sara sighed. 'Come on. Let's find somewhere to crash for the last ten minutes of lunch.'

Memphis nodded and followed her out of the classroom. 'And then it's French. Be still my beating *coeur*.'

On their way out, they passed by the school office reception. The big-boned frizzy replacement was still behind the desk, looking flustered and unhappy as she spoke to an inquisitive teacher.

'Yes, I *did* phone the hospital,' she said. 'The nurse has only got a mild concussion, he'll be back in school in a couple of days. And yes, the real receptionist *was* meant to be coming back at lunchtime but, no, I don't know where she is. Why should I?'

  136

'*I'm only a temp!*' Sara mouthed along with her as she and Memphis reached the main doors.

Outside there were still little huddled groups of traumatized students, clutching their stomachs and looking deathly pale. Mad rumours were flying around. One of the canteen helpers had an accident with a hand blender and blended their hand—that was where the fingers and thumbs came from. Others claimed that the detached digits were placed in the food supply by vegetarian terrorists. Still others reckoned that a murderer had been disposing of his victims in school dinners—people had been eating bits of them ever since the start of term.

The only rumour Sara actually believed was that the Head was calling an emergency assembly last lesson. Figured. If people went home looking the way they did now, he'd probably find about twenty lawsuits on his desk by tomorrow morning.

'At least we'll miss Maths,' sighed Memphis.

'Well, I still think we should tell a teacher,' said Sara.

'About missing Maths?'

'About what we know! Maybe we could leave an anonymous note.'

137

'What, pointing the finger at Colin Cox?' Memphis still didn't seem convinced. 'Wait and see how Sam got on first. He may have persuaded him to confess or something.'

Sara nodded to a red-faced, unkempt figure straggling along the path towards them. 'Here he comes now.'

But just a few metres away from them he veered off to see someone else; someone who Sara hadn't noticed in the crowd.

Sara was gobsmacked. 'Why's he wasting time on Ruth Cook again?'

'You look a right state, Innocent,' Ruth crowed. 'What's up—come to beg me to show mercy to your nerdy girlfriend?'

'Aw, come on, Ruth,' said Sam. 'Why should we argue? How about we make up. How about a hug.'

She stared at him. 'You *what*?'

'There's too much hate in the world,' Sam proclaimed. 'Let in the love, Ruth!'

Sara's jaw dropped lower as Sam threw his arms around Ruth in a kamikaze embrace. People laughed and whistled, pouncing eagerly on the distraction. Shocked speechless, Ruthless stood like a tree playing host to a deranged koala for several seconds before she regained her senses, broke Sam's grip and shoved him clear.

'He's mental!' she bellowed, and stalked away, red faced.

Sam ignored the ribbing and the jeering from those around him as now he continued on his way to Memphis and Sara.

'You look weirdly pleased with yourself,' Sara said.

'Just taking care of a little problem,' said Sam mysteriously.

'A dirty great big one, more like,' said Memphis. 'And she doesn't seem taken care of to me.'

Sara nodded. 'Yeah, what on earth was *that* little display about? And what's this about your nerdy girlfriend?'

'Jealous?' Sam asked.

Sara laughed. 'You wish!'

'Anyway, never mind Ruth's twisted imagination,' said Sam, changing the subject. He lowered his voice. 'I caught up with Colin in the end—and he didn't admit to a thing. I accused him, and he made out I'd got it all wrong.'

'He's got to be lying,' said Sara.

'That's the funny thing.' Sam looked thoughtful. 'I almost believed him. He seemed really angry about the whole thing.'

'Well, he just lost a big fight in front of half the school,' Memphis pointed out.

'Whatever,' said Sam. 'Since he won't come clean, I'll have to track down some hard evidence that says he's dirty. There's one place left to look, but it'll be dodgy.'

Sara sighed. 'Why can't you just give it up? If we tell a teacher—'

'You think that after all we've been through today I'm going to let a *teacher* step in and solve this?' He stared at her. 'Where's your sense of pride?'

'Out the window,' said Sara, 'along with my breakfast.'

'We've come too far.' Sam was adamant. 'We'll crack this thing ourselves. Like I said—I *hate* an unsolved mystery!'

'Looking at the state of you, they hate you right back,' said Memphis. 'So what are you going to do now, Sherlock?'

'I'm going to find my way to Horrible Hayes's room. To his book cupboard, to be precise.'

'You don't want to mess with Hayes,' Memphis warned him. 'He makes Penter look like a pussycat.'

'You mean he dresses him up?' joked Sam. 'Nice thought.'

Memphis sighed and got out a pen. 'Do you have your school site map? I'll mark the way for you.'

He couldn't find his, so Sara produced hers instead. 'OK, I'll bite,' she said. 'What are you hoping to find in Hayes's book cupboard?'

'That box we saw Ashley and Colin carrying out first thing this morning. That's where they were taking it. It was full of textbooks for some charity thing.'

'So?'

'So, I reckon Colin hid the thumbs and fingers inside it when Ashley barged into Penter's room and surprised him,' said Sam. 'Colin *hates* Ashley—and yet suddenly he volunteers to help him carry a big box of books halfway across the school. Why?'

'I smell a rat,' Memphis agreed.

'No, they were never delivered,' Sam grinned. 'You probably smell a decomposing thumb!'

'Speaking of which, it sounds like the Head's

calling a special assembly this afternoon,' said Sara. 'You know, about the lunchtime thumbfest.'

'He'll be looking for answers, fast,' said Memphis, handing Sam the marked-up map. 'But he'll probably settle for a scapegoat or two.'

Sara nodded and lowered her voice still further. 'So if I were you, Sam, I'd get that dumb digit out of your pocket fast!'

'Oh, don't worry about that,' said Sam with his trademark cheeky smile. 'I lost it already.'

Sam jogged over to the History block. He checked his watch—barely three minutes to go and lunchtime was over. If Horrible Hayes was already in his room, his own plan would be history before it happened.

Of course, Penter would be out for his blood by now—he hadn't done his lines, and he hadn't handed them in. But there was time to worry about that later. He *had* to get to the bottom of this mystery now—whether because of some weird recurring destiny thing or because he was just a nosy little git, he wasn't sure. But right now little else mattered to him.

 142

He found his way to Hayes's form room, which was spotlessly—almost frighteningly—clean and tidy. The floor gleamed, the books on his desk were arranged in orderly piles (and doubtless in alphabetical order), the boring historical scenes on the wall were all spirit-levelly straight . . . It gave naturally scruffy Sam the creeps.

But he was here on a mission. A walk-in cupboard was placed behind the teacher's desk. He crossed the room and tried the door. It opened without the slightest squeak—stood to reason the hinges were oiled regularly.

Sam flicked on the light switch—just as the squawking, hooting signal for afternoon registration blared out. He almost jumped clean out of his dirty, sweaty uniform.

He knew he should get out of here, fast, before anyone came in. He knew he should give up on this whole dumb detective bit before he got into *serious* trouble.

Instead he closed the cupboard door behind him. *I'll be dead quick*, he thought.

Among the neatly stacked boxes of scrappily-bound books, there was a large hunk of cardboard dumped hastily in a corner. Dark damp patches

143

dogged the box, as if something inside it had leaked.

Sam's heart quickened at the sight. For a moment he thought he could actually hear it beating, a rapid, tumbling skitter of clips and clops. Then he realized the room outside was filling with people. Maybe Hayes himself was one of them, bowling up to take the register.

While Sam was trapped in the cupboard.

Afternoon Registration

In Penter's form room, Sara eyed the empty spaces where Sam and Ashley ought to be. Penter himself looked to be possessed with a terrible icy calm. His red-rimmed eyes swept around the room.

'Has anyone seen Innocent and Lamb?' he enquired, stroking the patchy beard on his chin.

'Think they've run off together, sir,' said Ruth, earning herself a laser-sharp stare. Sara noted that the mousy girl beside her had shuffled her chair as far away from Ruth as possible, and was staring down at her desk as if she wanted to burst out crying.

'I received Lamb's lines,' Penter continued. 'They were stuffed under the staffroom door shortly before the lunchtime bell. But I understand he ran away from Miss Bedfellow's English lesson this morning. Can anyone shed any light on this?'

No one spoke.

'Mr Innocent, apparently, did not turn up at all,' said Penter.

Sara cleared her throat. 'He wasn't feeling well. And he wrote out his lines at lunchtime, but someone was sick on them.'

Penter bared his scabby teeth in a horrible smile. 'How very inconvenient.'

'It's true, sir,' said Fido Tennant, glancing over at Sara. 'I was there, saw it happen. Gross.'

'Me too,' added Memphis. 'You really wouldn't have wanted *his* lines pushed under the staffroom door.'

'Oh, very well,' said Penter, defeated by this show of strength.

Sara looked across at Fido and mouthed, 'Thanks.' He nodded his head a fraction and smiled.

'Please, sir,' Sara went on. 'Last time I saw Ashley, he was being sick. Maybe he still is. Sam wasn't feeling too clever either.'

'Well, I want you all to keep your eyes open for them,' said Penter. 'As you may have heard, the headmaster is holding a special full school assembly in period eight. And he means, *full*

146

school assembly. Absenteeism will not be tolerated.' His voice rose in sudden anger. 'I don't care if that irritating pair have to sit crouched over sick bags—they *will* be there!'

Sam peeked through the keyhole in the cupboard door. The class had quietened right down the moment Horrible Hayes walked in.

Hayes was one of those teachers who shouldn't be scary, but somehow was. He was a small, slight man, barely taller than Sam—but he had a presence about him that made you just shut up and respect. He wore square, thick-rimmed glasses that seemed to magnify his flinty stare, and his black hair—like his moustache and beard—was cut short and neatly groomed.

This was not a teacher you could give lip. This was not a teacher you could trip up. And this was certainly not a teacher you wanted to catch you in his cupboard when you had no business there.

Quietly, to the soundtrack of Hayes calling the register, Sam investigated the box with its tell-tale damp spots. The lid wasn't sealed, and he lifted it.

147

Inside there were dozens of history books. *Soggy* history books, cold to the touch. He lifted some out. The ones underneath were even wetter. He made a damp pile of them.

Searching deeper in the box, Sam's fingers brushed against something cold and hard: a metal case about the size of a small briefcase. He lifted it out and studied it—it was secured with two clasps, one of which was broken. Inside, the case was lined with thick plastic insulation, coated in icy slush.

A few stray fingers floated in the slurry.

He'd been right. Colin Cox was behind everything.

Sam stood back up, his excitement rising—and knocked over the soggy pile of history books he had so carefully stacked.

They made a dreadful din, collapsing like wet dominoes and thudding in a scattered pile against the door. Sam rushed over to try and gather them up.

But the door was already opening. The sodden books spilled out over a pair of very dark and very shiny black leather uppers.

Sam swallowed hard and looked up into a

148

dark, brooding face. Flint grey eyes were starting to twitch behind thick spectacles.

'Mr Hayes?' he asked nervously. 'Pleasure to meet you, sir.'

A muted wave of astonished chatter broke out among the class.

'That's enough,' snapped Hayes, and silence reigned once more. He bore down on Sam again, his voice dark and velvety. 'Who exactly might you be?'

'Sam Innocent.' He cleared his throat. 'Um, is this the charity cupboard?'

Hayes raised an eyebrow. 'It is.'

'Then . . . does that mean you'll treat me charitably?'

Hayes's grave stare was growing stonier all the time. Then, with a sinking heart, Sam saw why.

One of the history books had flopped open to reveal a severed pinkie.

'What unusual bookmarks you find in old textbooks these days,' Sam mumbled.

Hayes smiled, a full, fat, and satisfied smile. 'Well, well,' he said. 'It seems a culprit for today's unpleasantness in the canteen has fallen at my feet.'

'It wasn't me, sir,' Sam protested. 'I'm innocent!'

'Yes, so you said—Sam Innocent.' Hayes reached out a cold hand to help him up. 'But it would seem the finger of suspicion points to you!'

Period Seven

French

'Memphis, look!' said Sara. 'Ashley's right there!'

After his absence at registration, Sara had assumed the rest of the day would be Ashley-free. But he was sitting alone at a desk near the front of the class for Madame Rille's French lesson, sucking morosely on his thumb. His bag lay crumpled at his feet.

'Wasn't expecting to see you here,' she remarked. 'Feeling better?'

'I guess.'

'Thought you'd be lying low,' said Sara. 'Penter wants to talk to you. I think Miss Bedfellow told a few people about what happened in English—'

'I don't care!' hissed Ashley fiercely. 'I'm sick of running and hiding the whole time.'

Sara raised her eyebrows. 'Well, good for you.' She paused. 'I'm glad you got your bag back OK. You know, when Sam couldn't fetch it, me and

151

Memphis tried instead—only Roger stopped us. Thought we were trying to trick you.'

Ashley frowned. 'When did you see Roger?'

'In Bedfellow's room,' said Memphis. 'He picked up your bag and brought it to you in the loos, right?'

'No,' said Ashley. 'I wasn't *in* the loos. When I told Roger I'd run out of English, he told me to hide out by the caretaker's hut. So after what happened at lunchtime, I cleaned myself up and went there.'

'And he took your bag there?' asked Sara.

'He was asking about my bag at lunch . . . But he didn't offer to get it for me. I found it hanging up in the cloaks when I got back. My lines were tucked into the front flap. I thought Sam had put it there.' He looked around at the rest of the class filing in. 'Where is Sam, anyway?'

'He's pushed off. Wimped out,' said Ruth Cook, swaggering into the room. 'Shame on him. Leaving his poor little girlie friend to wait for her beating all alone.' She sniggered at Michelle Harris, who was looking haunted and pale in the far corner.

'Ruth,' said Memphis, 'I know you're totally

vile and everything, but do you have to be such a loser too?'

'Like anyone cares what *you* think, freak,' retorted Ruth, sloping off to her place beside the dozy ginger kid.

Sara looked at Memphis. 'So that's what Sam was trying not to talk about at lunchtime. Somehow he's got that girl into bother with Ruthless.'

'He's brought nothing *but* bother to just about everyone today.' Memphis led Sara over to a desk in the classroom's centre. 'While Roger's been bringing bags to Ashley in secret.'

'Yeah,' said Sara, sitting down. 'Why tell us Ashley was hanging out in the toilets?'

'To keep us away from him?' mused Memphis. 'Maybe he was just being protective.'

'Maybe,' said Sara doubtfully. 'Talk about a total overreaction.'

'*Bonjour, la classe!*' Suddenly a small, somewhat birdlike woman with bright eyes and straight grey hair flapped into the classroom. Madame Rille, Sara presumed. '*Ça va bien?*'

At that moment, Ashley jumped up from his desk and screamed.

Memphis stared. 'Speaking of overreactions . . .'

Madame Rille twittered to her desk in alarm. Then her eyes flashed with annoyance. 'Ashley!' she said in heavily accented English, trying to compose herself. 'Whatever is the matter with you, boy?'

'Look!' Reaching into his pencil case, he scooped out some thick, stubby objects.

Sara's mouth went dry. 'More thumbs!' she croaked.

The class broke out in uproar, some people screaming, others laughing, others just shocked. Ashley dropped the digits on his desk and grabbed his bag. While everyone looked on in disbelief, he shook it upside down.

Books fell out, a calculator, a magazine . . . and a further flurry of severed thumbs.

As they fell and bounced on to the floor, the room grew even rowdier. Ashley's neighbours scrambled clear of his desk. One boy jumped on a chair and screamed. Madame Rille's appeals for calm fell on deaf ears.

'*Shut up!*' bawled Ashley. '*All of you!*'

The stunned class fell silent as the grave. Even Madame Rille plonked down in her chair, mouth gaping.

'I won't be treated like this!' he insisted, both hands clenched into fists. 'I *won't*! I'm going to settle things once and for all!'

With that, Ashley stormed out of the classroom and slammed the door behind him.

Everyone looked at everyone else, dazed. Even Ruth Cook seemed stunned by the outburst.

Madame Rille kept opening and closing her mouth like a grey-haired goldfish, until finally she found some words. 'Class, I must report this boy's behaviour to the Head.' She walked warily past Ashley's desk and twittered to the door. As she vanished from view she called back, 'You will all stay here in your seats!'

Sara and Memphis looked at each other.

'Yeah, right,' said Sara. 'And miss this?'

'Let's get after him,' Memphis agreed. 'You know, this heat is making me so thirsty . . .'

Sara grinned. 'We need a drink of water or we'll faint!'

Fido Tennant leaned over from the neighbouring desk. 'Go ahead,' he hissed. 'I'll cover for you if Frilly Rille comes back and makes trouble.'

Sara smiled at him. 'You're all right, Fido.'

'What can I say? We dogs are such loyal animals.'

His own smile grew cheeky. 'So will you at least read my new screenplay when I'm finished?'

'Will *you* read my lips? N-O.'

He pretended to be heartbroken. 'A guy could go off you, you know.'

'Uh-uh.' Sara shook her head coyly. 'When a dog gives its heart, it's for ever.'

A moment later she and Memphis were heading for the door.

Sam had been stood with his nose to the chalkboard while Horrible Hayes concluded his registration. The alarm had gone for the next period, but while the class duly filed out, Hayes remained to complete some pieces of paperwork. Sam supposed being kept waiting in fretful silence with lungs full of chalk dust was supposed to unnerve him. Well, it was working. And he knew that this little mind game was just for starters—Hayes was really going to make him suffer.

'Right,' announced Hayes. 'I think it's time we had a chat with the headmaster, don't you?'

'Yes, sir,' said Sam. 'I'm looking forward to sharing my theories with him.'

'Theories?'

'Yes, of who's really responsible.'

Hayes gave him a cold, carefully measured smile. 'Ah, the optimism of youth.'

Sam was marched out of the classroom and into the courtyard outside. It was deserted of course, since lessons had already begun. But there was one figure running along who seemed familiar. Sam almost didn't recognize him with his thumb out of his mouth.

'You there, Lamb!' bellowed Hayes. 'What are you doing out of class?'

'I've got business to take care of!' snarled Ashley.

Hayes was outraged. 'How dare you speak to me like that!'

Ashley's only answer was to hurl something at Hayes before scurrying off on his way. Sam saw a small, severed thumb bounce off the teacher's chest.

'At least he didn't give you the finger, sir,' said Sam innocently.

'Ashley Lamb!' Hayes spluttered. 'You will stop running! Come here now!'

But there was no stopping Ashley. He beetled

up a flight of outside steps, and Hayes charged off after him in pursuit. Marvelling at this sudden change in the thumb-chum, Sam followed after him.

As he approached the upper floor of what was apparently the Humanities block, Sam saw Sara and Memphis cautiously enter the courtyard from the neighbouring building. 'Come on!' he hissed, beckoning them on. 'This is going to be mega!'

Sam took the steps two at a time—and reached the top in time to see Hayes turn left at a junction in the corridor. 'Ashley?' the teacher called uncertainly. 'Where are you, lad?'

Great—Hayes had lost him. Now was Sam's chance. He took a right instead, and followed the corridor round a dogleg in time to see Ashley throw open a door and barge into someone else's classroom.

'What's the meaning of this?' cried a surprised female teacher. 'This is my Personal Health class!'

'I know,' said Ashley. 'And I'm going to be very bad for *his* personal health!'

Sam arrived in the doorway to see Ashley striding towards a white-faced Colin Cox. The guy

just sat there, looking grim, as Ashley approached
. . . and walked right past him.

To attack his brother, Roger, seated behind.

'You've gone too far!' screamed Ashley, throwing himself at his older brother. The stunned class suddenly broke out in excited babble. Pens and books went flying as the struggling boys overturned Roger's desk and fell to the floor.

Ashley pummelled Roger's chest with his flabby fists. 'I'm not putting up with this any more! All right?'

'Get off him!' yelled the teacher over the crazed shouts of the crowd.

'Yeah, what are you playing at, Ashley?' said Sam. He pointed at Colin Cox. 'It's *him* you want!'

'Don't be so sure,' said Sara behind him.

'She's right,' added Memphis.

Sam turned to stare at them. 'Hey, you haven't seen Horrible Hayes anywhere—'

'Ashley Lamb!' roared Hayes, turning the corner behind them, his teacher radar drawing him to the noisy classroom like a fly to a turd. He pushed past Sam and Sara and Memphis, barely registering their presence. 'That is *enough*!'

 159

The class fell silent. Ashley seemed finally shocked to his senses, and scrambled back up. Roger, red-faced and glaring, got to his feet too. Both stood silently, heads bowed.

'I'm sorry to intrude, Barbara,' Hayes told the baffled teacher before turning to Ashley. 'And so will *he* be!'

Ashley's violence seemed spent. Now his baby-ish face looked about to burst into tears. 'But . . . but Roger has been taunting me with chopped-off thumbs! He's been doing it all day!'

'That's total rubbish!' cried Roger.

'I'm inclined to agree,' said Hayes. 'I've caught the boy responsible for spreading the thumbs.' He turned an evil eye on Sam. 'It's *him*!'

But Sara's eyes had fixed on something. She quickly charged across to Roger's fallen desk before anyone could stop her. 'Then how do you explain this?' she demanded—and yanked a blazer from Roger's bag. She shook it like a dusty rug.

A full handful of fingers tumbled out from one pocket.

Sam and Memphis exchanged revolted glances, while the Personal Health teacher slumped suddenly over her desk in a dead faint.

Hayes's eyes started twitching. 'Is this your blazer, boy?' he asked Roger.

'No, sir,' protested Roger. 'It's Colin Cox's! He nicked them in the first place!'

'You grass!' yelled Colin, and now *he* threw himself at Roger as the classroom erupted into fresh chaos. Sara tried to pull him clear, and Sam waded in to restrain Roger.

'There will be no fighting here!' bellowed Hayes. 'To the Head's office! All of you! *Now!*'

So, Sara, Sam, Colin, Roger, and Ashley were all marched away to the Head's office. Memphis had somehow managed to slip away —as ever, never caught up in events, always observing.

Well, she'd need X-ray vision to observe the climax to this weird little adventure. Hayes took them into a small room that must act as the Head's reception area, hidden behind a heavy wooden door. Madame Rille was coming out just as they went in. She muttered darkly in French and gave them a disappointed look.

'Wait here, you lot,' said Hayes gravely,

disappearing into the Head's office ahead of them. 'You will be dealt with shortly.'

The door closed heavily.

'This is all your fault, Ashley,' grumbled Roger.

'*His* fault?' Sam stared at him. 'How'd you figure that?'

'Him and his stupid thumb.'

'What about *your* stupid thumbs?' hissed Sara. 'You've got a bag full of them!'

Sam nodded at Colin Cox. 'I thought they were *his* thumbs!'

'They were, at first,' said Colin. He looked tired and defeated.

'Go on,' said Sara. An excited feeling fluttered through her at the thought of getting some reasons for all this at last.

So Colin began. 'It started when I was told to take a package for Cabbage Kale to Penter's form room by Mrs Willow.'

'We know,' Sam interrupted. 'You sometimes get a lift in with her, right?'

'She lives next door,' Colin admitted. 'Gives me a lift if I can't be bothered to walk to the bus stop. And she's got air-con in her car. The

162

whole world could be boiling outside, but it's like the arctic in there.'

'Which explains why you went with her today,' said Sara.

'And why you had a blazer with you,' added Sam. 'In case it got *too* arctic.'

'Anyway, I was mucking about a bit on the way there . . .' Colin sighed. 'I hate Kale, he's always piling homework on to me. No one was about, so I thought I'd kick his box around a bit, you know . . .' He paused. 'But it broke open.'

'And you couldn't resist taking a peep inside?' asked Sam.

He shrugged. 'It was a metal case, really cold. I thought maybe I'd broken it so I checked.'

Sam nodded. 'And you found it was full of fingers and thumbs on ice.'

'I nearly lost my breakfast there and then. I was just checking one out to see if it was real, when the door opened . . .'

'So you panicked and chucked the finger ice pop into the bin,' Sara realized.

'Yeah—I thought it was Penter or someone. And I quickly hid the case in the box full of old

163

history books. But it was just Ashley coming through the door—and he'd bccn told to take the box away!'

Ashley glowered at him. 'So that's why you acted nice to me and helped me carry it. You were worried I would look inside!'

'If you did, I knew you'd grass me up in two seconds to get me back for all I've done to you,' said Colin.

'Shows what *you* know,' muttered Ashley. 'I wondered why you wanted to stay in Hayes's room once we'd delivered the box there . . .'

Colin sighed again. 'I didn't know what to do. I should have just left the whole lot there, but I panicked, thought Hayes might unpack the books first thing and find the fingers.'

'He might have blamed *me*!' gasped Ashley.

'He'd have checked with reception,' said Colin, shaking his head. 'Willow would have told him *I'd* taken the package. I wasn't sure when she was going off to her appointment—I couldn't take the risk. So I scooped out as many as I could find, tore the packaging off the metal case, wrapped the whole lot up in that and shoved it under my shirt.'

164

'Cunning,' Sam had to admit. 'If Hayes found the case without any packaging, he wouldn't know who it was meant for.'

'Or where it had come from,' Sara agreed. 'That's why you took the delivery note too.'

'Then I made my biggest mistake.' Colin looked at Roger. 'I asked my so-called best mate to help me get rid of them!'

Roger looked surly but said nothing.

'We bunked off the start of first lesson, and I showed him. But he didn't want to get rid. He just eyed up the thumbs and told me it was a perfect opportunity.'

Sara frowned. 'To cause total chaos?'

'No,' said Roger, giving her an evil look. 'To cure my dumb baby brother of his thumb-sucking habit once and for all!'

Sam and Sara stared at him.

'So *that's* what all this was about?' asked Ashley quietly.

'You're nothing but a joke, Ashley!' said Roger. 'You may not care, but I do. It reflects badly on me! I'm always getting teased and stuff . . . I've spent years trying to get you to stop sucking that thumb!'

'So when you saw Colin's horrible haul, you decided it was time for shock tactics,' said Sara. 'You thought you could scare him out of the habit with those severed thumbs. Gross him out so much he'd never put a thumb near his mouth again . . .'

'It would have been a nice, quiet little terror campaign, and only Ashley would have suffered,' Roger agreed, scowling at Colin. 'But chicken-features here fouled everything up.'

'Good one!' Sam laughed. 'Chicken-features—*fowled* up, get it?'

Everyone glared at him and he shut up.

'What were you doing in the sickroom, lesson one?' asked Sara.

Roger opened his mouth to reply but Sam got there first. 'Getting ice packs,' he said. 'To try and keep the thumbs fresh. Right?'

'Didn't want them to thaw out too fast and start niffing,' said Roger, looking at Sara. 'Told the nurse I'd felt faint with the heat, so he let me lie down. When he nipped out to the loo it was the perfect chance to help myself to some ice packs.'

'But then I came in and disturbed you,' Sara realized.

166

Roger shrugged. 'When you opened the door, I thought it was the nurse coming back. I dumped the thumbs in the icebox and jumped back on to the bed.'

'And that's how blood got into the ice cube tray,' said Sara. 'Then you fobbed me off with a lie about your ankle and got me out of the way by sending me to fetch a bag that wasn't there.'

'Worked, didn't it?' smirked Roger. 'At breather, I got Ashley with the "Kick My Butt" sign on his back.'

'We thought it was Colin!' said Sara.

'I was just pushing him around a bit,' Colin protested. 'Ashley thought I liked him after I helped him with the box, and I didn't want other people thinking that!'

Ashley shrugged and then glared at his brother. 'So when I thought you were helping me, you were just slapping that sign on my back and slipping a chilled thumb in my pocket,' he said quietly. 'That was horrible of you.'

'I had to scare you bad!' protested Roger. 'Like curing someone of hiccups—it's got to be a big shock!'

Sara shook her head in amazement. 'So you hid the thumbs in Ashley's lunch when you stopped by his table to talk to him.'

'But why target everyone else in the canteen?' Sam wondered.

'That wasn't me! I didn't have anything to do with that!' said Roger. 'I didn't know that Colin had totally bottled out.'

'Well, why did *I* have to carry all those horrible things around with me, just 'cause I had my blazer?' Colin complained. 'Even with ice packs in my pockets they were thawing out and starting to smell . . .'

'Got it!' cried Sam. 'Ashley, remember when we were sneaking about outside the canteen during English? That dinner lady had just chased someone away!'

Ashley frowned. 'Colin?'

'I was trying to dump the fingers and thumbs,' he admitted. 'Too risky to leave them in one of the litterbins—the stink might have brought someone looking. But I thought if I could shove them in the kitchen bins, away from all the pupils . . .'

Sara understood his reasoning. 'No one would notice one more bad smell around the canteen!'

'Only you cocked up, didn't you?' sneered Roger.

'I dumped most of them in these big metal bins, before they chased me away.' Colin cringed. 'At least, I *thought* they were bins. Turns out they were food drums—one full of custard, one full of beans!'

'All that mess in the canteen really stole my thunder,' grumbled Roger. 'I knew Colin must be trying to get rid of the haul—so I went after him.'

'And that's why you nicked his blazer,' said Sam triumphantly. 'To get back any thumbs he hadn't managed to dump before he could try and get rid of them again!'

'And once you had them, you hid them in Ashley's bag,' said Sara. 'That's what you were doing when we came in on you. You'd never offered to get Ashley his bag. You didn't even want him to know it was you who'd returned it, in case he linked the thumbs back to you. You just left it in the cloaks where you knew he'd find it!' She could feel herself getting angrier. 'You hypocrite! You tore me and Memphis off a strip about trying to play tricks

169

on Ashley—when you were playing the meanest trick ever!'

'It was for his own good,' insisted Roger, turning to his brother. 'What I don't get is, how did you know it was me?'

'I'm not totally stupid,' said Ashley. 'Sara said you'd got my bag for me—and I knew you wouldn't do something nice without a reason. And when I found the thumbs in my pencil case, I realized it *had* to be you. You saw me at breather and I had a thumb in my pocket next period. You saw me at lunch and a minute later there are three thumbs on my plate . . .'

'I don't blame you for being angry with Roger, Ashley. I thought you were going to kill him.' Sam smiled. 'Bummer though, isn't it? When you're clenching your fists, you just can't suck your thumb!'

Ashley stared down at his fists in wonder. 'I . . . I didn't even notice!'

'See? The plan was working!' said Roger proudly. 'I'd have broken his stupid habit in no time—if other people hadn't interfered!'

'Maybe,' said Sam. 'But one thing's for sure— once the Head gets through with you, I reckon you're going to look like a bigger sucker than Ashley could *ever* be.'

Suddenly the door to the Head's office creaked open and Hayes re-emerged like Dracula from his tomb. 'The Head will see you now.'

Sara rose with the others, casting a *Here we go, then* look at Sam. But Colin pushed ahead of all of them.

'All this is down to me and Roger,' he said stiffly. 'Not them. I'll tell you everything you want to know.'

Hayes looked at him with dark, vengeful eyes and nodded very, very slowly.

'Good thing we'll hear the explanations all over again,' Sam remarked. 'It was a bit much to take in first time around!'

Sara agreed. 'Even when I could follow it, I couldn't always swallow it!'

Sam waggled his thumbs at her. 'Just be grateful you didn't swallow anything else at lunchtime!'

As for Ashley, his hands were thrust determinedly in his pockets as he marched into the Head's office—with his own head held high.

PERIOD EIGHT

~~Maths~~ FULL SCHOOL ASSEMBLY

Sam, Sara, and Ashley were dismissed just as the signal sounded for last period: set free, without punishment.

The Head was a man of few words, and most of them were repeats: 'disruptive', 'justice', and 'detention' figured a lot. As he sat aloof in his leather throne, his staring eyes, grey wispy hair, high forehead and full lips put Sara in mind of an old Roman emperor. How fitting, she thought. Those ancient rulers had decreed life or death over their subjects simply by raising or lowering their thumbs . . .

So the Head had listened in lofty silence as Colin told his incriminating story, and as Roger tried pathetically to justify his actions. And when they'd finished, he had solemnly announced that he had no choice: he would have to make an example of them both.

Sam, Sara, and Ashley were let off with warnings never to get involved in nefarious deeds again, and to report any strange events to their teachers in future like good little boys and girls.

Yeah, yeah, Sara thought, as she put on her gravest face and nodded in humble agreement. *As if.*

Roger and Colin were told to remain behind. They would accompany the Head on to the stage in the full school assembly to be held accountable. There was talk of letters to parents and even possible suspension—depending on their willingness to perform community service around the area. Both had agreed they would muck in and get their hands dirty.

'How right you are,' said the Head nastily, and Sara had sensed that emperor's thumb of his turning all the way down.

'All things considered,' said Sam brightly as they joined the crowds heading for the main hall, 'that didn't go too badly!'

'I'm just glad we're out of there,' said Sara.

'Me too,' said Ashley, his hands still screwed up into fists.

Sam had noticed. 'Do you realize you've had

that thumb of yours out of your mouth for more than half an hour?' he pointed out. 'Is that some kind of record?'

'Leave it,' warned Ashley. 'From now on I'm not taking stick from anyone. I've been a joke for too long.'

Sara tapped his fat little fist. 'Looks like you're ready to dish out a few *punch*lines of your own, huh?'

Ashley gave her a little smile. 'Maybe!'

With that he strode off ahead, pushing his way through the thronging people.

'Sudden transformation,' Sam observed. 'I bet when the dust has settled and he's calmed down, that thumb will plop right back into place.'

'Maybe,' said Sara thoughtfully. 'But maybe not.'

'Hey!' She and Sam turned at the familiar voice to see Memphis moving towards them, her smooth, shaved head bobbing above the sea of faces around her. She linked arms with them both. 'So you got out of the Head's office alive, huh?'

'He didn't throw us to the lions after all,' smiled Sara.

174

'Let us off with a lecture,' Sam added, and explained all that had happened as they walked on.

'Freaky,' was Memphis's only comment when he'd finished. It summed up the whole deal so eloquently, Sara couldn't help but grin. 'So everything ends up happy ever after, right?'

'Almost,' said Sam grimly as they approached the main hall. 'Look. Over there.'

Sara saw Penter standing by the hall doors. 'Don't worry. We got you out of handing in your lines, told him people puked on them.'

'Thanks,' said Sam, 'but I didn't mean him.'

And now Sara saw he was actually looking at Ruth Cook. The burly girl was walking just close enough behind Michelle Harris to be intimidating. Of course—at the end of this period she was due a kicking, and clearly Ruthless wasn't about to let her forget the fact.

Sam suddenly ran on ahead. Sara looked at Memphis, who only shrugged. They hurried after him, watching warily as he stood between Ruth and Penter.

'Ruth, there you are,' he said, all smiles. 'I was hoping I'd bump into you.'

She hovered by the doors and turned her usual glower on him. 'What do *you* want?'

'Yes, Innocent,' said Penter behind him. 'What *do* you want? Hurry up and take your place for assembly.'

Michelle Harris was holding back too. Her eyes were fixed on Sam's, as if silently pleading for help. But Sam ignored her.

'Ruth has my pen, sir,' he said.

She frowned. 'Huh?'

'It's a special red pen and I need it back.'

'He's lying, sir!' said Ruth fiercely.

'I see.' Penter leaned towards Sam, red-rimmed eyes boring into him. 'I spoke with the Head on his way in, and I've heard the gist of what happened. *He* may have found you innocent, Innocent, but as far as I'm concerned, you're not.'

'Sir?' piped Sara, stepping up beside them.

'What is it, Knot?' frowned Penter.

'What is *what* not, sir?' she asked brightly. 'Sorry, sir, when you said "Knot", I thought you were talking to me.'

'He was not,' said Sam.

'Was you, sir?' Sara blinked. 'I mean, *were* you, sir?'

176

'Knot, will you kindly stay out of this,' frowned Penter.

'Look, sir, can I go through to assembly, please?' Ruth was folding her arms and smiling thinly. 'The new boy's talking rubbish.'

'It's in her skirt pocket,' said Sam. 'The right one.'

'Him and the new girl are cracked. They're both bad news, sir.'

'That's enough from you, Cook,' said Penter. Then he frowned. 'Are you *sure* you don't have his red pen? Something seems to have left a red stain in your pocket.'

Sara's buttocks clenched tight as she realized what Sam must have done.

Almost in slow motion, Ruth reached into her pocket, a look of confusion on her face.

And everyone stared in disbelief as she pulled out a *very* manky-looking thumb.

Ruth stared at the thumb dumbly for a few seconds. Then she looked at Sam, speechless with rage.

'Oops,' said Sam. 'Not a pen. My mistake.'

Penter towered over her. 'So, we have a further accomplice, hmm?'

'No, sir!' she croaked. 'I never saw that thumb before!'

'I suppose it just happened to find its way into your pocket?'

'Someone put it there!' she squeaked. Then she turned to Sam. 'Him! It's him, sir! He gave me a hug and—'

'I did *what*?' spluttered Sam.

'He tried to hug me! There were witnesses!' Ruth turned to Memphis, hovering behind Penter. 'You saw him! Didn't you!'

Memphis looked baffled. 'Sorry. Didn't see a thing.'

'Cook,' said Penter sternly, 'you have been caught red-handed.'

'Or red-thumbed, at any rate,' murmured Sam.

'And I'm aware of your hostility to Ashley Lamb. I don't know what you were planning to do with that thumb, but I will see to it you never get the chance.' He produced a hanky and confiscated the digit. 'And I feel it only right you share in the same immediate punishment as Roger Lamb and Colin Cox.'

'Punishment?' Ruth swallowed hard. 'What's that?'

Penter smiled. 'You will help them clear up that dreadful mess in the canteen after school!'

Ruth's face twisted in terror as Penter gestured that she accompany him to the front of the hall. With a last spiteful look at Sam she trooped inside to meet her fate. Sara gave a mental cheer that there was some justice in the world—even if it took a little injustice to bring it about.

'So that's where you "lost" the thumb,' said Memphis, giving Sam an admiring look.

But it was nothing compared to the look Michelle was giving him. Her vacant stare had turned intense, her dark eyes wide and joyful. 'Thank you!' she whispered simply.

'Now we're quits,' said Sam gruffly. He quickly walked inside. But as he turned to take a seat towards the back of the hall, Sara caught the smile on his face he was trying so hard to hide.

HOMETIME

Sam, Sara, and Memphis held back as the excited, chattering crowds pushed out of Freekham High into the sun-scorched afternoon. The Head's assembly had given only the barest details of the background to the day's phenomenal events; but Sam and his new friends had been up close and personal throughout. They were in no hurry to escape now that the mystery was solved and the dramas resolved. There was still so much to talk about, to look back and cringe at. What had seemed a gross-out nightmare at the time had become a celebrated adventure.

Now, as they stood in the entrance hall, Sam and Sara regarded each other. Had it really only been that morning they'd first laid eyes on each other? Sam somehow felt as if he had known her, like, forever.

Memphis was watching him closely, a glint in

those sea-green eyes as though she knew what he was thinking.

'Samsara . . .' she said quietly, smiling like a Cheshire cat.

'Don't start that again,' said Sara.

Memphis shrugged. 'I'm only saying—'

'Yeah, well don't,' said Sam.

'Today has to have been the weirdest day of my whole life,' said Sara with feeling.

'Me too.' Sam wiped his brow. 'And the thought that we might go through more days like this . . .'

Sara shuddered. 'Don't even go there.'

'Hey, hey, hey!' Fido Tennant strolled up to them and smiled at Sara and Sam. 'Top day. *Howling* mad! You really must start school here again sometime.' He grinned at Sara. 'And you know, you can take me for a walk any time.'

'Down, boy,' said Sara.

Fido laughed and turned to go. 'See you tomorrow, guys.'

Then someone else called a more particular goodbye. 'Bye, Sam!' It was Michelle Harris, waving coyly at him as she walked out with the last stragglers, saved from a ruthless fate.

 181

'She can do "loud",' said Memphis, looking impressed. 'Who knew? She's always so quiet!'

'Sam must have turned her up,' teased Sara.

'Shut up,' said Sam. 'She needed a hand, and I gave it, that's all.'

'While poor, scorned Ruthless had to make do with just a thumb.' Sara grinned. 'You know, I reckon Michelle Harris is safe for a while. It's *you* who'll be top of Ruth's hit list from now on.'

'And boy, can that girl ever hit,' added Memphis.

Sam winced. 'Still, I bet she's elbow deep in multi-coloured custard right now . . .' He couldn't help but grin. 'I'm hoping a bit of community service will make her a changed person.'

'Uh, guys?' said Sara. Looking at the school office, she sounded uneasy. 'Speaking of changed people, and those in need of a hand . . .'

'Hey!' beamed Sam. 'It's Mrs Willow! The one who got everyone in this mess!'

'By trusting Colin Cox to be a messenger boy,' said Memphis.

Sam nodded. 'And by wanting to try out the finger surgery thing in the first place.'

 182

There she sat at the office counter, in all her fake-tanned, wrinkled glory. She seemed in a daze.

'She was meant to be back at lunchtime, remember?' said Memphis. 'Looks a bit peaky, doesn't she . . .'

'Probably upset that she couldn't have that pioneering, cutting-edge—and probably really dodgy—operation,' Sam said sagely. 'All the clinic's fingers ended up here, didn't they . . .'

Memphis nodded. 'So what exactly did the clinic get sent after that mix-up at the Cryo Lab depot?'

Sara looked worried and wary all at once. She crossed anxiously to the office, and Sam and Memphis followed her.

'Er . . . Mrs Willow?' said Sara.

'Have you seen Colin Cox anywhere?' she asked in a distant voice. 'I'm supposed to take him home after school.'

'He's been . . . um . . . delayed,' said Memphis. 'Are you all right?'

Mrs Willow was staring into space. 'My hand,' she said faintly.

Sam cleared his throat. 'Yes, I'm sorry about those comments earlier—'

183

'The surgeon,' she went on, not hearing him. 'He was very brilliant. But so very highly strung. He would choose *today* to have a nervous breakdown . . .'

Sara, Sam, and Memphis swapped nervous looks.

The receptionist sighed. 'It all started when a box of rats was delivered to him in place of the donor fingers he was expecting.'

She held up the missing hand.

It wasn't missing any more.

Not all of it, anyway.

There was a palm there. But in place of fingers were five wriggling, squiggling rats' tails.

'They took him away in an ambulance when he'd finished,' said Mrs Willow, staring at her new hand. 'The clinic's manager was very sorry. But the earliest they can put things right is next Wednesday.' She cocked her head and flexed her 'fingers'. The tails cracked out like little whips. 'You never know, they may have grown on me by then . . .'

Sam gave her a shaky smile. 'Uh, you know what? School's over, and we should probably be going . . .'

As one, the three of them turned and walked away, out through the main doors and on to the school drive. Once they were out of sight, their steady, purposeful stride soon turned into a mad scramble to get away. They only stopped once they'd reached the end of the drive.

'Did we just dream that?' asked Sam, panting for breath.

'You wish,' said Sara, clutching the stitch in her side. 'Eeeuw!'

'It could only happen around here.' Sara and Sam stared at Memphis as she collapsed into high-pitched, hysterical cackles. 'Only here . . . Only at Freekham High!'

185

Steve Cole spent a happy childhood being loud and aspiring to amuse. At school his teachers often despaired of him—one of them went so far as to ban him from her English lessons, which enhanced his reputation no end.

Having grown up liking stories, he went to university to read more of them. A few years later he started writing them too. Steve has also worked as a researcher for radio and an editor of books and magazines for both children and adults. *One Weird Day at Freekham High: Thumb* is his first novel for Oxford University Press.